PRESENTED TO

_____

FROM

K D Johnson

_____

DATE

Jan 21, 2022
_____

# KISSED BY GOD

## STORIES OF LOVE, LOSS & SURVIVING IT ALL

## THE UNSTUCK WRITERS COLLECTIVE

Find Your Voice | Speak Your Truth

ISBN: 978-0-578-99805-3

Publisher: Audible Voices, LLC

Authors: Andrea Anderson, Virginia Lee Fortunato, Shalondra E. Henry, Martha Jeifetz, Vanetta Mingia, Lin O'Neill, Kerri-Ann Pradere-Johnson, Stephanie Thompson and Shakenna Williams

Designer: Yvanamarie Mingia and Sarah Emery

Editor: Sabin Prentis Duncan, Fielding Books

Printed In The United States

Books may be purchased by contacting the publisher at
www.audiblevoices.com

# KISSED BY GOD

## CO-AUTHORS

Andrea Anderson
Virginia Lee Fortunato
Shalondra E. Henry
Martha Jeifetz
Vanetta Mingia
Lin O'Neill
Kerri-Ann Pradere-Johnson
Stephanie Thompson
Shakenna Williams

# CONTENTS

# ABOUT THIS BOOK

"Kiss Me and You Will See How Important I Am."
Sylvia Plath,
*The Unabridged Journals of Sylvia Plath*

When words are not enough, a kiss has the power to convey what cannot always be spoken. While on the surface, a kiss has the power to communicate a range of complex love emotions, it also has the power to kill, destroy and betray. A simple kiss, in all of its complexity, can bind our hearts together through the good and bad of life's journey like no other singular act can.

These were my thoughts when praying, meditating and deeply considering the name for this collection of short stories written by nine amazing women. I wrestled to find the common thread weaving each of their stories together. In the end, it was their collective kiss that left me speechless.

Each author approached this project with an openness of spirit that I not only admire, but expect from each writer I coach. In developing their stories, each of them fought their demons, pushed past their fears and pulled from the purest places in their spirits to give voice to pain, losses and life challenges they survived. It was a blessing to bear witness to their metamorphosis from scared aspiring writers to powerful, confident published authors whose stories undoubtedly will transform and heal lives for years to come.

It is for these reasons, I have the great pleasure of presenting the incredible voices of the UNSTUCK Writers Collective. Not only was it a privilege to compile this beautiful collection of healing stories, but I hope that in reading them, the freedom that comes from giving voice to the story that God has written on your heart becomes clear.

Eternally,

# story one

# SHE HELD THE BAG TIGHTLY

## VANETTA MINGIA

*BAM! BAM! BAM!* I didn't care that the one-inch heels on my brand-new black patent leather strap dress shoes struck the tiled floor hard while echoing loudly down the empty fourth-grade hallway. All the fourth-grade classes were probably on their way upstairs from the school assembly. They probably got held up because of the fight.

Yes, the fight!

Trouble had been brewing for the last two months, since when I first met Tanya and her flunky, Paulina. It started on the very first day at my new school. Right after the morning announcements, Mr. Dave, my first white male teacher, stood up and walked over to me. Placing his left hand on the back of my chair, he said, "Class, I want to introduce you to Camilla Gill. She transferred from P.S. 144 in New York." Before he could finish the introduction and feeling very proud of where I had been born and from which I had just recently moved, I corrected him, saying, "I transferred from Harlem, New York." Nodding his head in agreement, he smiled and said, "Yes, Camilla transferred from P.S. 144 in Harlem, New York. Please welcome her to our class." The students actually stood and clapped.

As I looked around the classroom, taking in the applause, making eye contact with my new classmates and feeling good, I saw lots of smiling faces. But as my eyes continued to scan the room, they got stuck on Tanya and Paulina. They were the exceptions. I looked at Paulina. She was looking at Tanya, who had her arms folded and her lips bent upward. She sucked her teeth and said,"Smuuk." Paulina stood there and mimicked Tanya's expression. She folded her arms and sucked her teeth too. She acted as if she were a puppet. I couldn't help but roll my eyes, and I eeked out a "Whatever," under my breath. Evidently, it was louder than I thought.

"So what, who cares if she is from Harlem?" Tanya said it loud enough for the class to quiet down. "What's so special about Harlem?" she continued. Mr. Dave interrupted the conversation right as I was just getting ready to reply and said, "Alright girls, have a seat." Tanya got the last word in, "Yeah, we are gonna talk later." Paulina repeated what Tanya said. Like I said, she was her flunky.

Every day when it was time for lunch, Tanya always had to be first in the cafeteria line, and Paulina made it happen. She didn't have to push kids out of the line anymore; they just stepped back, making room for her and Tanya as they approached. They were the class bullies. Some days during recess, I noticed they stood by the tall fence and stared at me. I wondered sometimes what they were thinking, but I didn't let it bother me. Several weeks after their comments about Harlem, all of which I had forgotten, I skipped over to them during recess and asked, "Do you wanna play tag with me and Marceline?"

Marceline and I had quickly become good friends. We had a lot in common. We were in the top reading and math groups together. We both brought lunch from home, oftentimes having peanut butter and jelly on the same day. We even had the same Bugs Bunny backpack. Most of all, she and I loved to race each other in the schoolyard at recess. Whenever the opportunity presented itself, we challenged each other to a full sprint. However, we weren't the only sprinters in our class. Mere hundredths of a second after our invitation to Tanya and Paulina, two boys from Mrs. Page's fourth-grade class sprinted over to where we were. Laughing as they ran past me, one of them grabbed the short, curly black wig off of Paulina's head and tossed it to the other, who threw it over the 12-foot fence. It happened so fast. I don't think anyone else saw it. Paulina instantly grabbed her top-knotted beige skull-hugging stocking cap, which covered her patchy bald spots, with two hands and ran after the boys.

I don't remember if Paulina caught them, but I do remember Tanya accusing me of being a part of the wig snatch. She said angrily, "You and Marceline tricked us, so the boys could snatch her wig!" That was far from the truth, but the wig-snatching was funny. I felt mixed emotions towards Paulina. I immediately started laughing at her which caused another problem. I also saw her sheer embarrassment and shame as she ran off chasing the boys.

Who knows if she chased them to protect her ego or because she was embarrassed that it happened in front of us? But I knew she couldn't catch them. They bolted and vanished into the sea of screaming and happy kids. The sounds of laughter and kids shouting at recess drowned out Paulina's screaming. We all knew she wore a wig every day anyway, but our laughter probably made her just want to run somewhere and cry. My laughing not only made me pee on myself just a little, but it also saddled me with a red bullseye, making me the target of Tanya's wrath.

Now, back to why I was headed to the office.

I purposely and angrily continued stomping my way down

two flights of stairs to the assistant principal's office. Tears blurred my vision as I gripped the staircase banister tightly with my right hand to keep from falling. I had twisted and held the now stretched waistband of my navy-blue pleated skirt tight to my waist with my left hand. This day was not going well. My reasons for crying were jumbled and swirling around in my head. Why were my tears so free-flowing? Was it a combination of missing my life in Harlem and adjusting to the new school or trying to fit in while making new friends? Maybe I was crying because I was in trouble for fighting in school. Was I worried that "Troublemaker" would be highlighted on my perfect report card? The only two reasons I could clearly make out from the jumbled mess of emotions and tears I was feeling were:

One - I just had a fight and
Two - My favorite skirt was ruined.

The closer I got to the office, the harder I began to cry. "Why am I being sent to the main office? It's not fair, I didn't do anything wrong. Just because I got sick and tired of being pushed, pulled and hit, I have to get into trouble? Why didn't Mr. Dave ever see Tanya or Paulina bothering me? It happened every day. How could he have not seen them or heard their petty conversations about me being stuck up because I lived in Harlem?" I said to myself taking in rhythmic gulps of air. "Maybe he was ignoring them and thought they would eventually stop bothering me and pick on somebody else." I used the sleeve of my bloodied wrinkled white assembly shirt to wipe my tears and my runny nose.

I reached Mr. Zigler's office. His door was open. His secretary said. "Go on in. He is waiting for you." I walked in. Holding my waistband, I smoothed the back of my blue and red-pleated skirt and sat down on the edge of the wooden chair next to his desk. My feelings of anger had now become feelings of anxiety, frustration and shame. Not waiting for him to ask me what happened, I started blubbering and couldn't stop. He pushed an open box of tissues toward me. "I didn't want to fight. I'm not a fighter," I said blowing my nose. It all came pouring out, every detail. I knew I was going to be suspended and my perfect school record would be ruined. He never interrupted me. I told him exactly what happened...

"When I raised my hand today at the beginning of the assembly trying to get Mr. Dave's attention, Paulina laughed, whispering loud enough for the other kids to hear, including me. 'Put your hand down, tattletale. You're gonna get your butt kicked today,' she said. Tyrone, the boy who sat next to me, put his hand over his mouth and said, 'Oooooohhhh! There's gonna' be a fight.'" A wave of nausea hit me and made me feel sick to my stomach. I wanted to throw up but held it down. "During the assembly, I couldn't sing the Star-Spangled Banner. I was mouthing the words to it and thinking at the same time," I shared with him. "Maybe I should try to negotiate with them. Maybe I should try to be their friend, but I didn't want to because I don't like them. They are bullies."

I was going back and forth trying to make a good decision, continuing to plead my case to Mr. Zigler. "Both of them took turns kicking the underside of my chair during the entire assembly. I felt every *thump, thump, thump* of their shoes. I turned around and said, 'Stop it,' only to see them laughing at me. I tried to ignore it. I tried to ignore them, but they didn't stop. I sat forward on the tip of the seat to lessen the shaking. They even tried to stretch and pull my skirt through the opening at the back of the seat," I sobbed.

Grabbing another tissue to blow my nose, I had begun to calm down. I had to pace myself. I knew this day was going to get worse before it got better. I knew the red bullseye had doubled in size and I was in big trouble. I continued with my side of the story, "At the end of the assembly, Mr. Dave walked to my row and said, 'Stand up class. It's time to head back upstairs.' And since my row was called first, that meant Tanya and Paulina would be walking behind me. I paused, "Mr. Zigler, can I have a cup of water?" "Yes," he replied. He got up and walked over to the water cooler. He pulled a white cone-shaped paper cup from the long silver dispenser, pushed the little white lever, and filled the cup with water. "Thank you," I said, taking the fragile cup carefully, trying not to spill water. I drank it all.

"Would you like some more?" he asked. I shook my head, "No," and continued. "As we walked up the aisle toward the swinging doors, I turned around and saw that they had moved up in line closer to me. I was really scared. They were going to beat me up. When they started pushing me, as I was walking up the stairs, my mind went blank and everything started to fade to black. I remember being pushed into the classroom and tripping. That was when I lost it. I turned around and snatched Tanya's white shirt by the collar and punched her in the face over and over again. We were on the floor, rolling in the front of the classroom. I remember holding onto Tanya so tightly that we rolled over the green trash can. I was yelling at her, 'I'm so tired of you always bothering me." I didn't know those boys were gonna snatch Paulina's wig.' I was crying and my nose was bleeding onto my white shirt when Mr. Dave pulled us apart. Everything had happened in a flash. That's when Mr. Dave said, 'Go to Mr. Zigler's office.'"

I stopped the story there. I knew not to share with him how I felt walking out of Mr. Dave's classroom, but I couldn't deny the feelings of strength and power that came with standing up for myself and fighting back. For just a moment, I felt this was the best thing that could have happened. I felt the red bullseye shrink. I had enough of being bullied. I just hadn't thought through all the consequences. I was in big trouble. Mr. Zigler said, "Sit here. I have to talk to Mr. Dave, make some calls and fill out a report." I knew I would have plenty of time to think about what I had done and how my life might be changing.

Sitting in the office gave me an opportunity to think about how I ended up here.

We moved from Harlem in August of 1982. I was not at all excited about attending fourth grade at a new school. I was already missing my old friends and my old neighborhood. But when my dad, the oldest of five kids, became focused on something, you couldn't change his mind. He was focused on moving and buying a certain type of house. He always said, "We need to buy an income-producing semi-attached house. It needs a separate entrance for a paying tenant." Then he would add, "Making and saving money is the way to financial freedom, and having a tenant will help us do just that." My parents purchased a nice brick two-family house with a porch on a tree-lined street in the Bronx. It had three bedrooms, one and a half bathrooms, a basement, a chain-linked fence around it, a wide driveway and a big backyard complete with thorny rose bushes and, of course, a separate entrance for the tenant.

I really liked so many things about the house, but I did not want my parents to know that they were right about buying it and moving us from Harlem. I loved having more than one bathroom. I loved sitting on the porch, especially in the rain. I loved running around in the rose-scented backyard. I even loved the driveway. We could play dodgeball in the driveway because the fence kept the ball from going into the street—well, it did when we actually closed it. Closing the fence was my responsibility along with my sisters. I hated that I was always the one who had to open and close the fence once the car was pulled out of the driveway. We were supposed to take turns opening and closing it, but my sisters weren't being fair. They often ganged up on me, and I ended up doing their portion of the work. "Camilla, it is your turn to close the gate," said Tessa. "No, it is not. I closed it yesterday." I shot back. "Yes, it is," Dani added. I hated arguing and I wouldn't have gotten my way anyway, so it didn't matter. I just closed the fence. I also shared a bedroom with my sisters, but thankfully, it was large and we all had our own beds. Tessa and Dani shared the bunk beds, and I had a day bed.

Shortly after arriving at our new home, I met some of the kids in the neighborhood. Edward and his two sisters lived six houses up on the same side of the street near the corner. Emily and her family lived next door to us. I met her first, just as the movers were unpacking our belongings and carrying them into the house. She stood on her porch and waved at me. I waved back. "Hi, I'm Emily! What's your name?" she yelled. "Camilla," I replied awkwardly, due to having never had a white neighbor before. "Nice to meet you. Do you want to play dolls?"she asked holding a white Barbie in her hand. "Maybe later," I yelled back, with a little more confidence. "I'm moving into my new house. It was nice meeting you. See you around." I instantly knew Emily and I would become good friends. She was friendly, just like me. Emily would eventually become my first Italian neighbor and friend. She didn't go to P.S. 78. Her parents sent her to the neighborhood Catholic private school. Between Emily, Edward, and his sisters, my introduction to the Bronx was going well. I hoped it would continue through the start of school.

Summer was coming to an end. My mom had arranged for us to visit and say goodbye to our neighbors who lived in our old building and have a final fun day with friends before the new school year started. We drove back to Harlem. We said our goodbyes to Mr. Jon and Mrs. Mari who lived on the third floor. They were both happy and sad for us to move away. They hugged me so tight, I could barely breathe, as they prayed that I would have a good life in the Bronx. I sure hoped their prayers were working now. They were moving to North Carolina in a month. My Harlem friends and I met at Mount Morris Park for our last day together. We climbed the rocks and played freeze tag. Together, we swung wildly on the swings for the last time. It was an emotional ending to my life in Harlem. There had been so many tears and hugs. We promised each other we would call and stay in touch.

My mom drove me to P.S. 144 to hug my teachers and have my school records transferred to the Bronx. The final stop was Mr. Ralph's Candy Store on 7th Avenue. I loved the candy store so much that it became my after-school hangout. In fact, Mr. R felt like a part of my family. It seemed like he had every penny candy in the world laid out in open boxes and in wide-mouth plastic jars big enough for your hands to fit on the long shelf that went from the front to the back of the store. After school on Fridays, Mommy would let me and my friends run down two blocks to his candy store. During our last visit, Mr. R was so happy to see me that he gave me a big hug. Mom told him we had bought a house and had moved to the Bronx. He told us, "Me and my wife are selling the store and retiring." We were really happy for him. He said, "Camilla, thank you for being my best customer." He handed me a bag of jawbreakers, my favorite candy, and said, "Be sure to share it with your sisters." I half agreed. "Okay, thank you, Mr. R." I gave him a big hug. "Bye," I said. Mommy and I left the store. It seemed to me that everyone was leaving Harlem.

Shortly after things were finally settled in the new house, dad found our new tenants, Mr. Joseph and Ms. Gwen. They seemed really nice. Ms. Gwen would sometimes babysit for us if mom and dad had errands to run. We didn't know any other people in the Bronx. They were referred to my dad by some good friends of his. The first day of school was approaching. My mom, Mary Ellen had just enough time to shop for me and my sisters at EJ Korvette's, a huge department store on Boston Post Road. She bought me three new outfits, two pairs of shoes and a Bugs Bunny backpack so that I would be ready to start school in style. My favorite outfit was the one I would wear every Thursday.

Thursday was the school's assembly day. Girls at our school were required to wear a navy-blue skirt with a white shirt. My blue skirt was fancy. It was pleated. My white shirt had a buttoned-down collar and came with a removable blue bow tie. When I tried the skirt on in the EJ Korvette's dressing room, I couldn't stop swiveling my hips back and forth to show the red inside when the pleats opened. I knew I was looking exceptionally good when I had on my skirt and when mom braided my long hair with red ball barrettes. She would braid my hair tight, but not too tight. I loved it when she added the barrettes. I could twist and turn my head at any time to make the *clickety-clackety* sound. But I learned to remove the barrettes before going to bed. Trust me, sleeping in them was painful.

Mary Ellen never missed walking her girls to school on their first day of classes and moving to the Bronx didn't change her routine. On our first day of school, mom called out, "Robby get the camera! The girls are ready." We lined up by birth order in our new front yard. I was in the middle. I was always in the middle. Posing dramatically with my hands on my waist, my chin and chest pushed out, wearing my red flare skirt, matching white striped shirt along with a big smile, I grinned as Robby took pictures of us with his Polaroid Instant Land Camera.

After taking the photos, we were ready to go. On my first day of school at P.S. 78, we walked the four blocks from Tillmann Avenue to Reedham Avenue. We passed Max's Minimart on the way. I wondered if he sold penny candy. "Mom, can we stop here?" I asked, looking up at her. "Sure, call your sisters." They had walked ahead of us and were waiting for us at the corner light. Yelling down the street, I screamed, "Tessa! Dani!

Come here. Mom said we could stop here to see if they sell penny candy." They ran back towards us, laughing. With their backpacks bouncing up and down on their backs, we all entered the store. Mom shushed us, "Shhhhh! Remember we don't touch things we aren't buying," she reminded us. I looked around the store. It was nothing like Mr. Ralph's store. Max's Minimart was big. It sold nearly everything. He had shelves and shelves of canned food and boxes of soap powder. Although I knew we didn't have much time, I also knew what I was looking for. There they were sitting in a wide-mouth jar on top of the counter. There must have been hundreds of them. "Look Mom! They have jawbreakers," I whispered, jumping up and down, pointing while jostling the contents of my backpack.

Living in the Bronx wasn't going to be so bad. Mom squeezed my hand and looked down at me. "Alright girls, it is time to get going," she said. As I skipped out of the store, squeezing mom's hand tightly, I waved goodbye to the man behind the counter and asked, "Is this your minimart?" "Yes," he said. "My name is Max." "Nice to meet you, Mr. Max," I said, pushing the door open, ringing the bell that hung above it.

The sound of the first lunch bell interrupted my thoughts. *Bonnnggggg!* it blared throughout the principal's office. Mr. Zigler walked back to his desk, sat down and looked at me. I could tell he was sad that I had gotten into a fight, but I knew he knew it wasn't my fault. He was quiet for a minute or two. Finally, he spoke, "I'm going to call your mom and tell her what happened. You won't be suspended for fighting, but you, Tanya and Paulina will have to meet with the school counselor until things are worked out," he said sternly. "Why do I have to meet with Mrs. Sanders? I didn't do anything wrong," I pushed back. "They have been picking on me since I got to this school. They don't like me, and I don't like them. Paulina is Tanya's flunky. Tanya tells her what to do and she does it. Last week, Tanya told her to pull up my skirt in the schoolyard in front of the boys. Ha! Ha! They didn't know I had shorts on underneath. She even tried to pull my ball barrettes out of my hair. Why does she wear a wig to school anyway?" There was still so much anger I needed to deal with, and Mr. Zigler knew it. He said, "You don't have a choice." With a small degree of resistance, I agreed to meet with the counselor and the troublemakers.

Mr. Zigler picked up the phone. He called my mom at work. "Hi! May I speak with Mary Ellen Gill, please? This is Mr. Zigler. Yes, I will hold." He spoke to her and told her all that had happened. As I sat there listening, I realized he had called both Tanya and Paulina's parents. They were both suspended for ten days, and their parents had to have a meeting with the school administrators and counselor before they could return. "Go home. Wash your face, change your clothes and be back in time for second lunch," he said. I was feeling so much better. I wasn't suspended, and to top it off, today's lunch was me and Marceline's favorite: a juicy hamburger and french fries, with a side of coleslaw and a chocolate chip cookie.

I left school and walked home. It felt weird leaving the building to walk home in the middle of the day, but I was kind of excited. I pulled out the key that hung discreetly around my neck to open the front door. After changing my clothes and washing my face, I called my mom. "Mom, I'm ready to go back to school. Mr. Zigler said I had to be back before the second lunch," I explained. She replied, "I'm very proud of you for standing up for yourself. We will talk more about it later tonight. I love you." But before she could hang up, I shouted, "Mom? MOM! Can I stop at Mr. Max's to buy some jawbreakers?" She answered, "Sure, why don't you buy enough to share with your classmates. Take some pennies from the penny jar." I shouted, "Thanks Mom!" and followed it with "Bye," before I hung up. As I headed out the door, I thought that I couldn't believe I had my first fight. I'm sure my parents never thought I would fight, let alone fight in my new school. I defended myself. That felt really good. I left home and walked to the store.

When I arrived, there were no customers in Max's Minimart. Stevie Wonder's "Master Blaster" was playing in the background on the boombox next to the register. Max was busy drumming his fingers on the counter to the beat and didn't notice me right away. My mood was matched by the jamming music. I was elated and full of excitement. While walking to Max's, I had been thinking about all the different flavors I would buy. I would get three red cherry, one for Marceline, one for Mr. Dave, and one for me. I loved sucking on the red cherry ones just long enough to make my teeth and tongue red and then rubbing it on my lips like I was putting on lipstick. After considering what flavors my classmates would like, I chose to get three orange, three grape, three green apple, and three lemon.

Because I was approaching the counter with a big smile on my face, Mr. Max knew what I was coming to purchase. He handed me the usual small brown bag. "Mr. Max, I need the bigger bag today," I said, picking up the silver tongs. "I am buying fifteen jawbreakers." After carefully putting fifteen in the square-bottomed brown paper bag, I twisted it tightly. I took a deep breath. The fingertips on my right hand tingled. I held the bag even more tightly as it began to feel a little slippery.

I couldn't help smiling. My cheeks were stretched across my face again. I heard the loud pounding of my heartbeat. My knees felt a little wobbly. The bag bulged with fifteen jawbreakers. "Dag! Fifteen jawbreakers!" I reveled in my thoughts. "You are here early. Is school over for the day?" asked Mr. Max, rudely breaking into my euphoria without permission. Quickly removing the wide smile from my face, my eyes dropped to the floor. Thinking for a moment, I said firmly, "No. I had something to do." I didn't want Mr. Max to know that I had been in a fight. I carefully laid the fifteen pennies on the countertop. Several of them were stuck on top of each other. Mr. Max counted them out and put them in the register. Even though I was excited, my mommy and daddy taught me and my sisters to keep our business private, especially when talking to strangers. You had to be smart to survive in Harlem, and Daddy would constantly remind his three girls, "Be aware of strangers." It wasn't Mr. Max's business why I was in the store early. I didn't know Mr. Max as well as I knew Mr. R.

I suddenly lifted my eyes, realizing I had been daydreaming again. Mr. Max was just standing there staring at me. He must have seen the excitement drain from my face. Awkwardly, he added, "Um, since you are a regular customer, you can take one extra."

"What?! A regular customer?" I blurted out in surprise. "I only come to your store on Fridays after school," I said, quickly adding, "Thank you." I slowly added one more red cherry jawbreaker to the already full bag.

"Bye, Mr. Max. Thanks again." Carefully pushing the mini mart door open with my other hand, I was tempted to run back to school but decided it was too risky with the bag being so full. I didn't want the bag to rip. I wanted to share my candy and tell my friends every detail of what had happened after Mr. Dave sent me to the office and that Tanya and Paulina were suspended for ten days.

So, I decided to stroll back to school. I didn't have to rush back and take the shortcut through the Reedham Garden Apartments because lunch wasn't for another 20 minutes. As I stood catty-cornered with my back in front of the Garden Apartments facing the school, waiting for the walk signal,

Paulina jumped from the path behind me and grabbed me, locking down my upper arms.

"Here she is, Tanya!" she yelled. Tanya walked up to me. I wriggled free of Paulina's grip. I wasn't scared anymore. There was no red bullseye. I had fought back. Tanya had felt my newly found strength. It was something she probably hadn't experienced before. Her pride was hurt. Her reputation had been fractured. Her face was bruised and swollen, and the collar of her white assembly shirt no longer laid down around her neck.

I held the bag tightly as I lifted my forearm. "You want a jawbreaker? I have an extra one." Even Tanya's pride couldn't resist a red cherry jawbreaker. I turned to cross the street, smiled victoriously and walked into school.

## ABOUT VANETTA

Vanetta is a mother of two and an educator with over 25 years of experience as a mentor teacher, administrator and classroom teacher. She enjoys running, taking long walks on the beach and flying kites. She takes readers back to her experience as a young girl in the fourth grade growing up in New York City public schools. With *She Held The Bag Tightly*, Vanetta gives readers a first-hand look at the challenges of attending a new school, making friends and dealing with bullies.

## ACKNOWLEDGEMENTS

I dedicate this story to my loving parents, Mary Ellen and Freddie Gilliam. They wanted only the best for their children and made many sacrifices to ensure our success and happiness.

# story two

# A DANCER'S HEART

## STEPHANIE THOMPSON

*"God will take away all the tears from their eyes. Nobody will ever die again. Nobody will be sad again. Nobody will ever cry. Nobody will have pain again. Everything that made people sad has now gone. That old world has completely gone away." Revelations 21:4*

JUNE 26

Today is the day. It is a surreal day. An unreal day. A heartbreaking day, a day that I never thought would be *my* day. Three questions continuously alternate positions at the forefront of my mind:

Why me?
Why her? and
Just why?

Even as those thoughts are replayed on an emotional loop, I can hear the soft murmuring of voices coming from downstairs, the constant creak of the front door opening and closing again and again. They were gathering. It was happening.

Meanwhile, I lay curled in a fetal position in the middle of my bed, on top of the covers. I can hear the chatter of my five-year-old nephew seeping through the bedroom wall, "Is she ever coming back?" I notice the childlike innocence in his voice. Although I strain to hear my sister's muffled reply, I already know the answer. She is not ever coming back. My heart aches with deep pain as tears silently roll down my face onto the brightly colored paisley pillowcase.

I curl into a tighter ball as I try to squeeze my knees up to my chest. She was my future, and now she is gone. The tears continue to flow as I weep, my whole body shaking. "Oh God," I think to myself. "How will I make it through this day? How will I make it without her for the rest of my life?" My mind is racing with so many thoughts.

Imani was my intelligent, beautiful, artistic, sixteen-year-old daughter. With her enticing warm smile, she was everyone's friend, a stranger to no one. She possessed a sweet, loving spirit that belied her age and endeared her to many, both young and old. She was a model student. Her teachers would always tell me, "I wish I could clone her. She is so kind and helpful to other students."

The love of Imani's life was dance. From age three, all she wanted to do was swirl and twirl, dancing her way across any floor, hallway, or room. She was tall, lean and had the perfect ballerina body. She ate, drank, and slept-dance. There wasn't a place she would rather be than in the dance studio or on-stage performing ballet, tap, jazz, or African dance. Our days together were filled with after-school rehearsals and weekend performances. She lived to dance and worked extremely hard to perfect her technique. She wanted to perform worldwide as a prima ballerina. "I am going to dance forever, Mommy," she would often say. I would laugh and reply, "If anybody can do it, you can!"

Raising her as a single mom had not been easy. Juggling swim lessons, dance practices, and softball games along with my hectic work schedule had been exhausting. Yet, I loved our busy, on-the-go life. I often took Imani with me to work and on work trips. I remember a particularly fun trip we took to Miami when she was five years old. It was the Fourth of July, and we watched fireworks on Key Biscayne. We also visited Sea World, where we were splashed by Orca the Whale. Imani talked about that trip for years! Because we spent so much time together, we were extremely close, and she shared a lot of her teen life with me. I was excited that she trusted me with the interior details of her life, from her secret boy crushes to her dance and school challenges and other juicy tidbits. We both gushed over the good news that she had been selected to attend the Governor's Honors Program. Only the top one percent of Georgia's high school students were selected for this honor. I was very proud of her.

That memory caused me to shift in bed as my thoughts began drifting back to the day my life changed forever.


JUNE 15

It was Tuesday morning, after we had dropped Imani off at the Governor's Honors Program in Valdosta, GA. I was leisurely getting ready for work when my phone rang. It was 7:30 am. "No one usually calls me this early," I thought to myself. Not recognizing the number, I answered the phone. "Ms. Thompson?" a male voice inquired. "Yes?" I questioned back. "My name is Ken Harris, the residential director at the Governor's Honors Program," he responded. "Why is he calling me?" I thought nervously to myself. "Imani has collapsed, and she is en route to the hospital. You need to get down here as soon as possible!" As my heart pounded in my chest, tears began to form in my eyes. I dropped to the floor on my knees and asked him, "Is she conscious?" "Yes," he replied. "I am on my way. Please call me if anything changes," I said hurriedly, feeling a bit relieved, although I was frantic. My fingers shook as I called Imani's dad, Dirk. When he answered, I screamed into the phone. "Imani collapsed! Imani collapsed! We have to get to Valdosta!" I briefed him on the situation and told him I was on my way to pick him up. I calmed myself just enough to throw some clothes into an overnight bag and rushed out the door. "I just need to get to her. I just need to get to her," I kept repeating to myself.

My mind was like a runaway train. I was imagining a million different scenarios. "What had happened since we texted yesterday?" I wondered. I ran through the facts as I knew them, even as my thoughts continued to tumble over each other. She told me that she had visited the infirmary. They ran some tests, said she had an infection, and they had given her some antibiotics and muscle relaxers because her shoulder hurt. She said she felt renewed and was better. "What happened?" My thoughts crashed into each other with fear and confusion, making me unable to make sense of it all.

My mind flashed back to the previous week. For several days, Imani had been suffering from a fever and a swollen finger. I had taken her to the doctor three times over a four-day period, including a trip to the emergency room. I wanted to make sure she was okay before we left for the Governor's Honors Program. Each time we visited the doctor's office, they ran a battery of tests, but could not find anything wrong. "A virus," they said. "It just needs to run its course," they reassured me. I trusted their opinion. After all, Imani was healthy and rarely ill, except for an occasional bout with childhood asthma, which she had seemingly outgrown by age eight.

Imani was ecstatic about going to Governor's Honors for

dance. She was packed. Her hair was freshly braided, and although she was not her usual peppy self due to the lethargy caused by her fever, she was relieved that she had gotten clearance to attend the program. At sixteen, this would be her first time away from home for more than a week by herself, other than occasional visits with her grandparents. She was thrilled about this new chapter of freedom and independence. As her mom, I, of course, was a nervous wreck for the exact same reasons.

## JUNE 13

On the day we were supposed to leave for Governor's Honors, Imani still had a low-grade fever, but she said she felt good and that she wanted to go. I gave her medicine and we left much later than planned. The three-hour trip seemed to take forever, and we were all anxious since it appeared that we would miss our scheduled check-in time. Imani dozed most of the drive down, and I periodically checked with her to see how she was feeling. She was excited, but a little lethargic. We finally arrived at Valdosta State College and soon found her assigned dormitory. The first person we met was the resident advisor. Through our introductions, we discovered she was a college senior and a nursing major. I was thrilled and relieved. I explained to her, "Imani has been experiencing a fever and the doctors believe it is a short-term virus. She has medication, but can you please monitor her and call me if something changes?" "I will definitely keep a check on her," the resident advisor promised as we finished unloading Imani's belongings. After unpacking Imani's clothes and arranging the dorm décor, Imani was anxious for us to leave as soon as parent orientation was over so she could join the other students.

Before Dirk and I left, I said, "Let's take this one last picture." We took the picture in her dorm room, surrounded by all of the newly placed purple décor. We all smiled brightly but were sad at the thought of leaving each other. I pulled Imani into my arms and told her that I loved her and asked her to call me if she did not feel better. At the time, I didn't realize that it would be my last hug and the last picture that we would ever take together.

## BACK TO JUNE 15

As we raced down Interstate I-85 from Atlanta to Valdosta, we replayed the events of the last 24 hours. I had texted with Imani, and her father had actually spoken to her. He said she had assured him that she was fine and had rushed him off the phone because she was watching *Project Runway* with some friends. We were convinced it was the muscle relaxers that had caused her to collapse. Several times along the way, the nurse from the emergency room at the hospital in Valdosta called us because Imani wanted to speak with us. We both talked to her, reassuring her that we were on our way and coming as fast as we could. Although she was talking to us, we had no idea what she was saying. She was mumbling incoherently.

Finally, we pulled into the emergency room entrance in Valdosta and ran to the reception area."We are the parents of Imani Twine. Where is she?" I shouted. The nurse looked at us sympathetically and pointed her hand down the long hallway. "She's in Room E3," she said with a sad smile. As we quickly rushed down the shiny linoleum hallway, I noticed that for an emergency room, it was eerily quiet and there was hardly any activity. As I pushed open the room's double doors, I stopped so quickly that I almost fell over as I saw her lying in the hospital bed. She was covered from the waist down in white sheets. It was apparent that she had suffered a stroke. The left side of her mouth drooped down, and her left hand was twisted in a weird, paralyzed-like position. I suddenly remembered the time my aunt had suffered a stroke and how she struggled to walk and talk again. But this time, it was happening to my baby.

I rushed to Imani's side as tears ran down my cheeks. "Hey Mani," I whispered softly into her ear. "Mommy's here," I crooned. As her face contorted in pain, she said, "Mommy... Daddy... what took you so long?" My heart broke at her words. I ran blindly from the ER room as the doctors and nurses continued to attend to her. Little did I know those would be the last words she spoke to me as they rushed her out of the room for yet more testing and another MRI.

Waiting for test results was tortuous. We were informed that during the second MRI, Imani had another massive stroke. "We have to airlift her to Shand's Children's Hospital in Gainesville for brain surgery," the doctor told me. "Surgery is needed to relieve the pressure on her brain from the strokes," he said. I immediately collapsed on the floor. "This is not happening!" I screamed as my mind broke under the weight of trying to process it all.

I started gasping for air and sobbing uncontrollably. "Oh my God! Oh my God!" I moaned as I started praying silently for God to save my child. I couldn't catch my breath as my body convulsed in agony. The nurses lifted me from the floor, into a chair, and gave me water. "Breathe," they said, "Just breathe." As I sat in the chair, trying to take in big gulps of air, I calmed a little, but all I could think of was Imani and her face grimacing in pain.

As they made arrangements to airlift Imani to Shand's Children's Hospital, I asked if I could accompany her on the flight. They refused because of liability potential. I was frustrated, angry and did not want her to be alone again. The flight took thirty minutes, but it would take us an hour and a half to drive the hundred miles there. Her dad and I hopped in the car at 5 pm to continue on the unknown journey that had started that morning at 7:30 am. We arrived at the hospital and were directed to the Pediatric Intensive Care Unit (PICU), which would become our home for the next seven days. We were briefed by the attending physician that evening. He was a kind, young doctor who mentioned that they were prepping Imani for surgery and would come back and let us know her status once they were finished. So much had happened in the 12 hours since I had received that initial call from the residential director.

The waiting for the conclusion of the surgery was endless. I thought about so many what-ifs. "What if we had gone to the doctor one more time? What if we had not decided to attend the Governor's Honors Program? What if I had stayed in Valdosta for a few days rather than leaving after we dropped her off? What if I had taken her to a different doctor? Maybe I should have gone to another hospital? What if? What if? What if?" I could not control my thoughts. I was scared, confused, and angry. Pangs of guilt racked my body and my mind. It was torture. "Why had I not seen this coming? Why didn't I protect my child better? " The thunderous waterfall of questions and second-guessing persisted throughout our wait.

## JUNE 16 – 1:00 AM

As Imani's dad and I sat in the small private waiting room of the PICU in the wee hours of Wednesday morning, all was quiet except for the hum of the television on the wall and the occasional hospital announcement over the intercom. No one else was in the room but us. Finally, a doctor entered the waiting room. His face held a solemn expression as he shared the news that Imani was out of surgery and stable. My heart swelled with hope. He explained her prognosis as, "If she wakes up and can say, 'My name is Imani,' then she will be okay." "When can we see her?" I asked nervously. I was so anxious to see her, hold her, and just be with her. He told us to wait until she settled into her room from the recovery area. My best friend, Linda, and her daughters arrived, and my heart soared that we did not have to handle this alone. Our support system had arrived. They immediately helped us begin to communicate Imani's condition to other friends and family, while also helping set up the prayer network of supporters for Imani.

## JUNE 16 – 4:00 AM

We finally got to visit Imani post-surgery since arriving in Gainesville. Her eyes were closed. Her head was wrapped in bandages. She was hooked up to all kinds of machines, including an IV, a ventilator to help her breathe, a heart monitor, a stomach tube, and blood pressure monitors. She even had on compression socks to prevent blood clots. The room was freezing. There were tubes everywhere. The constant *beep, beep, beep* of her heart monitoring machine was nerve-racking. With each beep, my heart leaped as well, anticipating each sound and praying that it would not stop. Her hand was still twisted in a claw-like position by her side. They instructed us to talk to her because sometimes unconscious patients can hear even if they can't respond. I rubbed her braided hair, caressed her beautiful face, and told her I loved her at least one hundred times. My repetitive reminders, "Mommy loves you so much," were all my heart could muster.

## JUNE 16 – 7:00 A.M.

After spending time at Imani's bedside after the surgery, we left the hospital to change clothes and take a quick nap. Fortunately, we had family friends in Gainesville who lovingly opened their home to us. I was exhausted physically and emotionally. I had no idea what was next. All the doctors could tell us was that Imani had a heart infection called endocarditis.

They were still running tests to get more information. "What was this monster illness that had taken over my baby's body?" My heart was painfully writhing with so many unanswered questions. I took a brief nap and was eating breakfast when the hospital called and said they wanted to meet with us at II a.m.

JUNE 16 – 11:00 A.M.

As we re-entered the PICU Unit at II a.m. to meet with the doctors, we were escorted to a small conference room down a narrow corridor not far from the entrance. I sat next to Imani's physician, who we had met yesterday, the pediatric neurosurgeon who performed the surgery, and the chaplain. Imani's dad, Dirk, and my best friend, Linda, joined me, taking their seats next to mine. The neurosurgeon started talking about brain capacity, brain function, and irreversible brain damage, but all I heard him say was, "The Imani that you know and love is gone." I immediately collapsed to the floor and began crying, wailing and screaming, "No! No! No! I took her to the doctor!" I sobbed. "I took her to the doctor!" I screamed at him. "Why? Why? Why didn't you stop this from happening?" I kept yelling and wailing until they threatened to hospitalize me. I thought my heart was going to explode and felt as though I was having an out-of-body experience. Imani was gone? What?! My loving, beautiful, smart, intelligent, and talented daughter is gone? Through tears, I asked him, "How could this happen?" The neurosurgeon calmly looked at me and replied, "Her doctors were looking for horses, but this... this was a zebra. This is such a rare occurrence in a child so young." He paused before adding, "The only part of Imani's brain that is working is the brain stem." He looked at us to gauge if we were following him. "So you have two choices," he shared. "You can put her in a nursing home with a feeding tube and breathing tube for the rest of her life or not."

I was numb. This was a nightmare of the worst kind. My head was throbbing so hard it felt like it was going to burst. It was all too much to process. All my life, I had lived in a metaphorical Pleasantville, where everything was sunshine and roses. "What about Imani's senior year and her dance performances? She had just been elected to the Student Council. We had prom plans and, of course, there was college. What about her wedding? As an only child, she wanted to get married and have lots of babies. What about all the life we had left to live?" I sobbed as I watched our plans fly through my mind's eye.

"Take your time to make a decision," the attending doctor said. "How could I even make such an impossible decision?" I wondered. Neither choice would lead to the future of which Imani had dreamed.

## JUNE 17- 9:00 AM

After spending that night at Imani's bedside, the next morning I found the hospital chapel and decided to pray. I was lost. I had a decision to make and only God could tell me what to do. I begged and pleaded with Him to heal her and restore her body. I even bargained with Him to take my life instead of hers. She had so much more life to live and so much more to accomplish. I needed a message from Him.

I spent all day lying on the chapel floor praying and talking with God. Meanwhile, family and friends had driven down to Gainesville from Atlanta to support us. My brother, my cousins, and Imani's friends and their parents all gathered in her hospital waiting room to visit with her and to keep vigil for some sign of improvement or brain activity.

## JUNE 18 – SECOND OPINION

A few days later, after conducting a family huddle on the next steps, we solicited a second opinion from a different team of doctors. I wanted to know beyond any reasonable doubt what Imani's quality of life prognosis would be with most of her brain capacity destroyed. What were her chances of regaining consciousness and being able to talk, walk, think, or reason? I had to know, medically, what the possibilities were and were not.

After meeting with the second team of doctors, we knew there was no hope. They confirmed the prognosis of the original physicians. Imani had minimal brain activity except for the brain stem, which controlled her breathing, digestion, and heart rate. All of her cognitive abilities were gone. A new diagnosis was also revealed-an infection called Group B strep, which was mostly found in pregnant women and seniors. Less than 5% of teenagers were infected with the disease.

It all began to come together for me. Group B strep was the cause of the infection that caused the endocarditis, which led to the infected blood being pumped throughout her body, including her brain, which ultimately caused the strokes. More questions gathered in my mind. "Where did the Group B strep originate? How long had she had it? Was it contagious? The physicians were able to answer some, but not all of my questions. By the end of the day, more than fifty family members and friends had gathered at Shand's Children's Hospital to pray for a miracle.

## JUNE 20

Several days passed with no change in Imani's condition. There was constant prayer and visitors traveled in and out to see her and support me. The hospital allowed me to lie in her bed with her, and I held her as best as I could amidst the tubes and other medical paraphernalia attached to her small frame. I sang to her. I read the Bible to her and made her promises. I promised Imani that I would work the rest of my life to honor her. I promised to promote her love of dance whenever and wherever I could. I also promised to carry her forgiving and loving spirit with me forever. One particular evening, as I was softly talking to her, a single solitary tear rolled down her cheek. At that moment, I knew she had heard me.

## JUNE 21

After much prayer and after receiving medical opinions from all over the Southeast, we decided to see if Imani's brain stem, which controlled her breathing, would allow her to breathe on her own. If so, then we would move her back to a facility in Atlanta. At 12:05 pm, the breathing tube was removed and she fought valiantly to breathe on her own for several minutes. As I held her hand and her dad held her other hand, she took her last breath and peacefully slipped away. The machines stopped beeping, and the doctor looked at me and nodded. This beautiful creature with a smile like sunshine and a heart full of love was gone. My heart instantly shattered into a million pieces. At that moment, I realized that part of me died as well. I instantly wanted to go wherever she was.

## JUNE 26

A soft knock on the door interrupts my thoughts. "Stephanie?" a male voice asked softly. "Yes?" I answered, recognizing my dad's deep baritone. "We need to leave for the church in thirty minutes," he said. "Okay, I'll be ready," I answered. But I wasn't ready, and I'd never be ready for this day. I slowly pulled myself out of my ball and began to get dressed, as I continued my reverie on the events that led me to this day.

The time has come. As I open my bedroom door to go downstairs, I face the first major step of my new reality – Imani's memorial service. Nothing ever prepares you for the death of your child. There are many things in life that I can handle, but I wasn't prepared for this. I never saw it coming. I now know that most parents are not prepared to handle such a devastating event. It is not the natural order of life. I was supposed to go first.

I want that unconditional love again. I want to hear her calling to me, "Moooommy," in that sweet voice again. I will have to cope with the fact that I don't have that anymore. I feel weak. I'm lonely and needy. I am no longer the self-assured, confident woman I once was. Yet, as I remember the gift of a lifetime called Imani, I am grateful for her love. The time I spent with my daughter was the closest my life has ever come to perfection. It sometimes seems like it was all just a beautiful dream.

I don't think we realize that life gifts us with amazing moments that add up to a lifetime of memories. I will honor Imani with my memories of love and keep those promises I made to her in the hospital. As her mother, I pray that God will somehow let our spirits connect again, not to continue any earthly connection, but to perhaps allow us to embrace as warm spirits connected by a timeless bond. I will never recover from the loss of her, but I hope and pray that I can make her loss meaningful.

∾

As I step out of my bedroom, I glance towards Imani's empty bedroom, take a deep breath and slowly walk down the stairs.

EPILOGUE

To honor Imani's memory and her amazing, but short life, I started a non-profit organization called A Dancer's Heart to provide scholarships and life skills workshops to help your girls and teens succeed. Imani's legacy continues. Here I am 11 years later, surviving, thriving, yet still missing my sweet girl. I am forever grateful to Imani's friends and my village, who continuously surround me with love and support. Imani's dad, Dirk Twine, recently passed away, and I pray that she was able to welcome him amongst the angels. Love Lives Forever. For more information, visit adancersheart.org.

## ABOUT STEPHANIE

Stephanie Thompson grew up in North Carolina, where, as the daughter of a minister, she learned the importance of serving and loving others with an open heart. After losing her only child, Imani, to a rare illness, she founded *A Dancer's Heart, Inc.*, an Atlanta-based non-profit to honor Imani's memory. The organization's mission is to help young women succeed, primarily through scholarships and life-skills programs. Also, after experiencing additional losses of family members, Stephanie became passionate about helping others move forward in their grief journey and is a certified grief counselor. She is an avid hiker and travel enthusiast. A Dancer's Heart is her first published work.

## ACKNOWLEDGEMENTS

Much love and thanks to my sister Dee, BFF Linda, nieces, nephews, and other family members and friends who have loved and supported me through this journey.

# story three

# ERASURE

## ANDREA ANDERSON

*"It's fair to say that black folks operate under a cloud of invisibility... This invisibility - this erasure out of the complex history of our life and time - is the greatest source of my longing."*
— *Carrie Mae Weems*

*L*aila Allen felt powerful. She radiated energy, dancing in front of the mirror and singing along with Alicia Keys' "Girl on Fire" while getting ready for work.

Today was going to be a game-changing day for Laila. She sized herself up in the mirror, smiling as she saw the confident, smooth, dark chocolate reflection staring back at her.

If there was a checklist for confidently good-looking, Laila checked all the boxes. Her makeup was flawless. Her naturally curly hair was pinned up into a sophisticated chignon with tendrils perfectly framing her face. Her feminine, modern, sleek red Carlie Cushnie designer dress made just the right statement-that statement affirming that this girl was indeed on fire, particularly because red had always been her power color. Yes, she was definitely ready!

After months of creating the perfect new innovative design for her firm's biggest client, today she would present some of the most extraordinary work she had ever done. Work that would undoubtedly make her a senior partner at the top architectural firm in the city.

Laila sashayed through the glass doors of the IDS Tower, catching a glimpse of her professional appearance as she headed to the elevators for her office on the 27th floor.

The office was abuzz more than usual for a Tuesday morning, with some of that buzz unknowingly focused on her. For eleven years, Laila had been working at the firm, and for a number of those years, she had been the only black female junior partner. Like the industry, the firm was predominantly male with all-white managing partners. The senior partner level was roughly the same, with the exception of one white female and one Asian male.

Rumor had it that the managing partners were looking to add another name to their letterhead, which could create an opening amongst the senior partners. An opening that today's presentation would all but guarantee Laila would earn.

Laila's journey at the firm had been an arduous climb, despite her talent and superior design skills. Her work was consistently praised by clients, and she was well-liked by her peers and staff for her leadership and ability to cross-functionally motivate project teams to greatness. Yet, when it came to promotion to the upper ranks, she was often overlooked. She was frequently made to feel as if she were invisible. But today? This girl was on fire, as all the presentation attendees would soon recognize. Alicia Keys was still singing in Laila's head as she gathered the materials for the big presentation from her desk.

"Laila, do you have a minute?" Senior Partner Diane Frost asked as she walked into Laila's office and closed the door. "I've been speaking to the managing partners and they felt it best that I make the presentation today. This is a huge project, and the partners feel like a more senior presence is warranted."

"What?" was Laila's immediate thought as the doors of opportunity were slamming shut.

"But, I'm totally prepared and have been working with the client for months. The client is expecting me to be there." Laila answered as she felt her temperature rise. "No disrespect, Diane, but are you even up-to-speed on the project and the client's needs?"

"Don't be absurd. Of course, I am. I reviewed your files last night and they are meticulous as usual. Your assistant is loading your presentation for me in the conference room now," Diane responded with a flip of her stiff bleached-blonde hair and a crooked smirk before exiting the office.

She peeked her head back in to add, "Oh and Laila, your presence is not needed at the meeting," Diane said, piercing Laila with her cold-blooded deep blue eyes. "There's a problem on the Wesson project that I would like you to spend the morning figuring out, and I'd appreciate it if you got right on that!"

"What the fuck just happened?" Laila muttered loudly under her breath. She wanted to scream but didn't want to draw any embarrassing or unwanted attention to herself.

She was certainly on fire now! If she was a dragon, she would spit flames and torch Diane and the state-of-the-art conference room in which she was about to present stolen ideas. Laila was furious! Diane's presenting and taking credit for work that didn't belong to her was becoming a nasty habit. Laila was not the only aspiring woman who had had her work intercepted by Diane, who did so as if it were her right, a privilege for which she bore no shame. For Laila, this was the second and last time she would be robbed by Diane.

*Bzzzzzzzt... bzzzzzt... bzzzzzt*

Laila was suddenly jarred from her heated thoughts by the ringing of her phone.

"Hello."

"Hey sis," came the ever cheerful and supportive voice of Laila's best friend, Olivia. "Today's the big day! From my mouth to God's ears, you've got this!"

A long silence followed as Laila struggled to find the words to speak.

"Laila ... Laila are you okay? Talk to me, you're making me nervous. Say something!" Olivia shouted in a concerned voice.

Laila finally found her voice as heated tears began to stream down her face.

"I'm not doing the presentation. It was taken away from me. That's all I can say right now or I'm going to freaking lose it and we both know I can't afford to do that here at work."

"Not that bullshit again. Jackasses!" emphasized Olivia.

Laila quickly wiped the tears from her face and regained her professional composure before telling Olivia, "I have to go fix a botched design on the project of the Judas who stole my account. We'll talk more tonight."

"I'm praying for you, sis. See you tonight. I'll bring dinner and Tequila with Friends," Olivia said soothingly.

Laila drove home, deep in thought. She had somehow managed to put on her Black Super Woman mask and pull it together enough to save the Wesson project. If that wasn't enough, she also virtually met with two prospective clients before deciding to walk out of work 12 hours later. Despite the pandemic, the construction and design industries had been deemed essential and continued to operate daily, following state and health procedures. Protocols, processes, and the way work was getting done changed daily, and it felt like it took twice the amount of energy to get through the day. She was exhausted.

She had called Olivia at 6 pm, letting her know she would be working late and to not bother coming over tonight.

"Those people don't deserve you," was all Olivia had said before hanging up.

Four hours later, Laila walked into her own spacious, beautifully decorated sanctuary and dropped her keys and purse on the counter. She grabbed a bottle of water from the fridge before aiming the remote and turning on the TV. She had been so caught up in her own traumatic day that it had suddenly dawned on her that she had no idea what had happened in the world today.

She dropped down on her comfy platinum leather sofa and kicked off her heels. She unpinned her long, curly hair and ran her fingers through it, massaging her scalp before letting her head drift back onto the pillow. Then, as the images on-screen came into focus, she bolted upright in horror. The video replaying the tragic murder of a 46-year-old black man, George Floyd, who was begging for breath, handcuffed and lying face down with white Minneapolis police officer Derek Chauvin kneeling on his neck. The officer knelt on his neck for nine minutes and 29 seconds as bystanders looked on in disbelief and anger as the scene unfolded. Floyd's last words, "I can't breathe," had never had more meaning. And it seemed that bystanders on the street and across the country had never felt more helpless as they watched this man's distress culminate in his imminent death.

Laila grabbed her phone and immediately called Olivia. "Are you seeing this?"

"Yes! It's unreal. The continued erasure of black lives from police brutality is horrific and inhumane," said Olivia in a dejected tone.

The faces of so many black lives began to flash through her mind like a morose award show paying tribute to fallen stars whose lives had been unjustifiably extinguished. The sorrowful montage of faces included Eric Garner, Michael Brown, Tamir Rice, Philando Castile, Atatiana Jefferson, Ahmaud Arbery, and Breonna Taylor.

Laila sat rigidly on the edge of her couch with countless faces running through her mind on a continuous loop when suddenly she felt a powerful, engulfing tidal wave of emotions rush over her. So powerful, that she was thrown off-kilter, oblivious to what Olivia was ranting on about over the phone.

"Hey Liv, I'm going to have to call you back!"

The news coverage continued. When Laila stood to race to the bathroom, she suddenly froze in her tracks, laser-focused on an interview clip of Patrisse Cullors, co-founder of the Black Lives Matter movement, saying,

*"I have never felt the grips of patriarchy and its need to erase black women and our labor... so strongly until the creation of Black Lives Matter."*

Cullors' words hit Laila at her core. Something about them resonated with her in a way that was so personal it was intimate. Like a bolt of lightning it hit her, jolted her, in fact. That was it. The feelings of being erased felt all too familiar. As a Black woman what she had been experiencing the past three years of laboring at her job was indeed her own erasure.

The many frustrations of her visionary leadership, ideas, and strategies were erased by white male senior partners as they blatantly took credit for themselves. And today, it had happened again, but this time she had been betrayed by a thieving white woman, determined to get ahead on the back of a black woman. The events of what had happened today at work and the outrage surrounding George Floyd's murder now had the frustrations she had pushed down deep inside of her boiling. That anger was now rising, bubbling over and pouring out in the heated tears that streamed down her face as she screamed, "Enough!"

What she realized in this space, at this moment, was that she had been wounded and had slowly been bleeding out the past three years from being overlooked and dismissed while sitting at the table. She realized she had been hurting in the in-between as she had continued to operate day after day in a cloud of invisibility and systemic oppression. The revelation that she too was slowly being erased triggered uncontrollable wailing.

Something within Laila snapped, and emotionally she came undone in the middle of her living room. She fell to her knees and began to weep in anguish. She called out to God in despair.

*Father God, I come to you broken and in despair, unable to breathe from the crushing pressure of it all. The pandemic, the social injustice, the systemic racism are too much!"* Laila prayed. *"How could you let this happen? I thought you loved me. I've put my faith, my career, and my life in your hands. And yet, I feel the stabbing, excruciating pain that surely accompanies bleeding out in death. I am drowning and in great need of rescue, of your saving grace.*

As her prayer gave way to sobs, Laila heard the soft whisper of God wrap and comfort her spirit like a snugly warm blanket. The whisper said,

*Laila, my child, let not your heart be hardened, for you are loved. You are a gift, and I am with you. I have created and instilled in you the talents and fruits of the spirit to be a warrior for justice, equity, and inclusion for yourself and others. Shrink for no one.*

*Become invisible to no one. Be erased by no one. You exist for a great purpose. Use your voice to rise up. Stand up and evolve into the masterpiece that I created you to be. Let the love and light dwelling in you shine bright enough that others might see it.*

Laila opened her eyes and rose from her knees with an unexpected sense of purpose and an understanding that she needed to funnel her emotions, her pain, and her voice into the fight. She realized that He was asking her to do a hard thing. God had whispered to her to be a force of change--a change that was apparent the next day at work.

Unconcerned with the feelings of confusion, condescending questions, and pure ignorance of her many colleagues at the office surrounding the murder of George Floyd, Laila left work early. She didn't have the strength or desire to counsel their over-privileged souls or educate them on the disparities felt by blacks who had watched friends and family die of coronavirus at higher rates, not to mention the insane number of blacks being pulled over and gunned down by police while driving, jogging or sleeping due to systemic oppression and racism. And she definitely was not interested in teaching a course on what to say or not say when white people encountered or spoke to other black people during these times. For years, Laila had smiled, silenced her rage, and assisted the upper echelon of white privilege by working twice as hard for less than half the pay.

"No more!" she thought. "There were books and highly overpaid so-called experts for that who, surprisingly, did not look like her. Let them deal with it!"

Laila headed out to join her two closest friends, Olivia and Jessica, in a peaceful protest that started at 1 pm. She was running late because she had stayed at work longer than planned to once again put out a fire created by one of the senior partners. The number of fires she put out on a daily basis around that place likely qualified her to apply for a job as a firefighter, maybe even a fire captain.

Laila arrived at the protest and was astounded by the vast number of people who had shown up. She stood in the middle of the street amongst the crowd, wondering how in the world she was going to find her friends amongst the many people wearing face masks. Suddenly, she heard a loud explosion. Her head swung in the direction of the booming sound to discover that the police were using tear gas grenades in an attempt to disperse and push back the growing crowds. People began running in all directions. She initially thought it was to escape the gas, but quickly realized the cause was something even more treacherous—rubber bullets. The police were firing rubber bullets at the protesters and at her. That realization paralyzed her where she stood. She didn't move. Couldn't move. It was as if she was rooted in that spot until someone collided into her and knocked her to the ground, causing a stray bullet to miss her by mere inches.

When she hit the ground, Laila briefly had the wind knocked out of her. As she struggled to regain her breath, she became aware of the intoxicating scent and feel of the stranger sprawled on top of her. She opened her hazel eyes with flecks of gold and green to the deepest, richest pair of brown eyes she'd ever seen. Those compassionate eyes were staring back at her as if they were looking into her soul. The owner of those intriguing eyes asked her, "Are you okay?"

"Yes."

"Good, because we can't stay here. We've got to move fast," said the six-foot-three, bald, muscular, dark-skinned stranger as he rolled off of her and jumped to his feet, swiftly pulling her up with him in one smooth motion. "Can you breathe? We need to make a run for it."

Laila nodded her head in the affirmative and the stranger grabbed her hand and began sprinting away from the chaos and commotion that had ensued as the police tried to protect and occupy their space.

The moment the gentle giant took hold of her hand, an electric surge passed between them sending tingles through Laila's body. The energy between them was electrifying, and the chemistry was unexplainably instant.

When they were a few streets over, the strong, towering, handsome stranger came to a halt. He turned and looked affectionately at Laila without speaking, giving them both a chance to catch their breath.

"Are you sure you're okay?" he asked. "My apologies for tackling you back there, but you seemed disoriented, and you were about to be hit by one of those rubber bullets. And while they are not real, they still hurt like hell and can cause some major damage. I couldn't let that happen to you."

"Thank you!" Laila said. "Chivalry is not dead. I can't believe that you put yourself in the line of fire and were willing to take a bullet for me."

"Yeah, well, I'm a sucker for a beautiful lady."

"You can't even see my face. How do you know I am beautiful?"

He laughed and said, "I'm an alpha male with a good eye. I have a sense for these things. Plus, your mesmerizing soulful eyes when we hit the ground confirmed you were worth it."

Laila blushed at the handsome stranger whose skin reminded her of chocolate fudge.

"Thank you again for coming to my rescue. I'm Laila."

"It was my pleasure, Laila. My name is Donavan Alexander III, but my close friends call me, Tre."

"Were you at the protest alone or was someone looking for you?" Tre asked.

"I was supposed to be meeting up with my friends. I was running late and had just arrived when all hell broke loose. I guess I should check my phone," Laila replied.

Laila pulled her phone from her small black leather cross-body bag and noticed she had missed four calls from her friends and a slew of text messages.

She immediately hit return on one of them, and Olivia answered after one ring.

"Laila, where are you? Are you safe?" Olivia asked. "Please tell me you are not at the protest rally!"

"No, I'm safe! I had just arrived and was looking for you and Jessica when things took a turn for the worse," Laila explained. "Thankfully, I was rescued by a black knight and I am safely a few blocks away. What about y'all?"

"I got caught up at work. I never made it,"Olivia replied. "I spoke to Jessica. She and her son are safe. When the first tear gas grenade was dropped, TJ got his mom the hell up out."

"Oh thank God! Everyone is safe!" Laila exclaimed in relief.

"Uh, what is this about a black knight?" Olivia teased. "You know, you didn't think you could just brush over that comment with your PR friend, did you? Give me the story!"

"I will later, let me get home first," Laila said, eager to get off the phone and get home.

"Um hmm... but only because I'm still at work and he's probably standing right there," Olivia teasingly said. "I'm going to give you time to get your story together, but it better be good."

"Bye sis!" Laila said as she disconnected the call and looked up at the smiling stranger. "What's so amusing?" Laila quipped as she turned her attention back to Tre.

"Nothing. Sounds like everyone is safe and I was wondering if you would treat a brutha to a drink. I mean, I did just save your life," stated a self-assured Tre.

"Okay, who's being cocky and dramatic now?" Laila flirtatiously bantered.

"Not cocky. Just confidant. Like my name, my warrior skills

speak for themselves." Tre boldly stated, "Now, can a brutha get to know you better or what?"

Again, Laila blushed behind her mask and consented to his request.

"Where's your car?" Tre asked.

"I left it parked at the IDS Tower," Laila specified.

"Great, I'll walk you back to the building and we can grab something to eat and sit in the Crystal Court," Tre replied.

The two engaged in easy conversation along their walk back to the IDS Center and all throughout the afternoon and well into the evening. Each person shared their purpose and reason for being at the rally. Expressing their concern regarding social injustice and connecting on an even deeper level on the black experience, Laila learned that the two shared a mutual faith in God and each opened up to share intimate details about their divorces and their pasts.

Tre was an industrial engineer by day, but a renaissance man at heart. He was also a true gentleman, a scholar, a writer and a musician. He played the guitar and the piano. He also rode a motorcycle. His greatest achievement, admittedly, is being a single parent to two exceptional children, who are in college.

Before they knew it, dusk had settled. They had been so absorbed in each other's company while sitting across from each other in the courtyard that the hours had flown by.

"As much as I have enjoyed talking to you, we'd better get you home. The city is under a curfew, and I think we've both been on the wrong side of the law enough today," Tre joked before winking at her.

He walked her to her car, opened the door and gave Laila his mobile number. He then made her promise to call him the minute she got home so that he knew she was safe.

Laila nodded, took off her mask, and smiled at him for the first time without it from behind her car window. Her smile and the twinkle in her hazel eyes took his breath away. Suddenly, Tre was having trouble breathing, and it had nothing to do with his mask.

## THREE WEEKS LATER

Laila awakened thinking about Tre and their late-night FaceTime conversations. The two had fallen into the routine of talking to each other every night since they met. A huge smile spread across her face just thinking about how much she enjoyed having his baritone voice be the last thing she heard before drifting off to sleep each night. He was quickly becoming a habit that would be hard to kick.

Laila's phone vibrated, signaling a text.

"Good morning, beautiful! Today's the big announcement. The next time I see you, you'll be a big-shot senior partner. I'm confident of that."

Dragging herself out of bed, Laila quickly dressed for work and headed out the door.

The managing partners had gathered the entire office together in the firm's spacious, picturesque, modern, sleek conference room with etched floor-to-ceiling glass walls.

"Today marks a momentous occasion. As we have the great pleasure of announcing the newest managing and senior partner promotions."

Diane smugly sat at the front of the room, ready to quickly stand and take what she felt was her rightful place next to the two named partners, Bill Tate and John Reynolds. When suddenly, she couldn't believe her ears.

"Join us in congratulating our newest partner, David Gardner, and his protégé, senior partner Luke York."

Stunned by the announcement, Diane was in such a stupor

she could barely bring herself to clap. "How is this even possible? I've done ever despicable deed you have asked and then some," Diane blurted out, piercing Bill Tate with a cold-blooded icy stare. "Worst of all, I have disrespected, stolen from, stepped on, and stabbed other women in the firm in the back to be one of the boys. And for what?"

Upon hearing the announcement, Laila exited the back of the room and headed straight to her office, infuriated that she had been overlooked once again. The good ole boy network was alive and well, and it was on full display. Luke York had been given, not earned, the senior position because of the coattails he was riding, not because of his talent. He couldn't design his way out of a box. Laila knew this first hand because she often saved his ass on projects they worked on together.

Laila's head was about to explode. If she got any hotter, she would combust and cease to exist for real. She grabbed her purse and left a message for her assistant that she was not feeling well and would be out for the rest of the day. She had to get out of that office. She couldn't breathe.

Laila raced from the elevator doors outside into the fresh air where she quickly yanked her mask off as the hot tears began to roll down her face. Laila could not suck air into her lungs fast enough.

She was tired of being wounded and pretending that she was okay. The reality of the situation was that she was not okay and had not been since May 25th, that fateful day when George Floyd lay in the street gasping for breath with his oppressor ignoring his pleas. The worst part was that nobody at her job had even bothered to ask if she was okay. And now, Laila simply didn't have the words to articulate why she was angry and grieving.

After sitting on a bench under a tree, calming herself for a moment, she pulled out her phone. Typically, the first person she called would be Olivia, but at that moment, the only voice she wanted to hear was his.

"Hey, sunshine! How's my baby the new senior partner?" Tre answered with a smile in his voice.

As silence hung in the air, Tre suddenly realized this was not the joyous occasion he had anticipated.

"Laila, sweetheart... You okay?"

"No, I'm not okay," Laila wailed. "I've been overlooked again. The good ole boys network lives on."

"Laila, I see you. I have since the day we met," Tre soothly stated. "Do you hear me? I see you! All of you!" he exclaimed. "There is nothing and no one who can take away your light or your talent. Do you hear me?"

"Yes, I hear you," Laila quietly whispered.

"You my dear, are the sun!" Tre replied before being interrupted by the ringing of his office phone.

"Laila, I'm getting called into a meeting. Are you going to be okay until tonight?" he asked.

"Yes, I just needed to hear your soothing, deep voice. Don't worry about me," Laila assured him. "I'm headed home. Call me tonight."

While driving home, Laila realized the state of her soul. After this morning, she was not at rest and could no longer be quiet. There was a fire raging inside of her.

## LATER THAT EVENING

Laila exhaled in the company of her best friends, who had arrived at her home to console her. Since the COVID-19 lockdown, they have created a ladies' night-in which they affectionately call "Wine Down Wednesday."

Olivia and Jessica safely social distanced around Laila's living room, intently listening to her replay what had happened that morning as she shared how she was feeling. They were having a lively discussion on how the biggest crime black women committed against themselves was shrinking and how shrinking to fit places you've outgrown was a first-degree offense.

Laila confided in her friends that she had outgrown the prestigious design firm of Tate, Reynolds, and now Gardner.

"I'm done!" Laila announced.

"It's time for me to stand tall, be bold, and go out on my own."

And as if on cue, the ladies noticed that the song playing in the background was Diana Ross' "I'm Coming Out." The three quickly jumped to their feet and began to dance around and sing along. They alternated lines and sang the chorus in unison.

Laila was grooving to Diana's melodic voice when she heard a knock at the door. She danced her way over to the door with her red wine in hand and opened the door to discover Tre standing with a concerned look on his chiseled face on the other side of the door.

"Hey, sweetheart! Don't be mad. I respect our COVID safety measures, so I had a rapid test done. I'm also not trying to move us along too fast, but I couldn't just call or FaceTime you tonight," Tre said, his worried eyes conveying his concern while giving Laila the feels at the same time.

"I had to see you tonight. Not only did I need to see you, but I also needed to hold you. I needed to know that you were really okay."

Laila sat her wine glass on the floor, flung herself into his arms and began to sway to the music as her friends looked on, mouths wide open.

"Oh, alright now! This must be the Black Knight!" Olivia emphasized as Jessica burst into laughter.

"Come on in here, baby," Olivia teased. "I don't know why

Laila has you standing outside in that unbearable heat. Doesn't she know chocolate melts?"

Laila gently took her man by the hand and pulled him inside to meet her best friends. Shortly after, Olivia and Jessica decided it was time to make their party of four a party of two as the sultry sounds of Marvin Gaye's "Sexual Healing" played in the background and Laila and Tre became lost in each other's eyes.

## THE NEXT MORNING

Laila awakened the next morning with a renewed purpose. She phoned the office and informed them that she would not be coming in. Because she had been a slave to work, she had banked over eight weeks of vacation, and it was time to put some of it to use. She would spend the next week meeting with her financial planner and considering her future in the comfort of her own home.

Laila's days were quiet and peaceful. Her mornings were spent with God, and her nights were filled with the baritone of her Black Knight's voice.

It was during her morning prayer that she was struck by the realization that what she wanted was to be able to breathe, feel alive and enjoy what was right in front of her - the man she had always dreamed of and the enterprising opportunity of a lifetime.

Through prayer and stillness, over the next few days, she was able to breathe life into herself. She learned to exhale the toxic injustice and turmoil that had been pent-up inside of her and inhale newfound peace. She was becoming spiritually fit.

Laila was sipping her favorite salted caramel mocha latte while journaling one morning when she received a call from not one, but two, of the firm's top clients, inquiring about her sudden absence. They wanted to know if she was okay. It was so not like her to leave, especially not for vacation, without giving anyone on her team a heads-up. They were genuinely concerned about her, but also expressed concern about the chaos and lack of competent service on their accounts during her absence.

The next day, Laila received a call from Bill Tate, the founding partner who had taken a chance on her in the very beginning by hiring her as a summer intern. He asked if she could come in right away. They needed to talk.

Hanging up, Laila sighed and rolled her eyes. She dressed in all black, as if in mourning, and went into the office. The minute she stepped off the elevator, she could feel the tension. In her mind, she could hear the imaginary *clickety-clack* of the hamster wheel, creating a dizzying whirlwind as soon as she stepped through the office door. For sure, she would not miss this nonsense.

She let Mr. Tate's executive admin know that she was there at Tate's request.

"Laila! Come in. Sit." Tate said, motioning for her to come in and get comfortable.

"How was your vacation?"

Laila sat quietly and let both of them linger in the long uncomfortable silence before speaking.

"It was great up until it was interrupted by me being summoned to the office for no apparent reason." She paused before adding, "With all due respect, sir, I think we both know this is not about my vacation."

Tate cleared his throat, as sweat began to bead across his forehead.

"You're right. It's not. Laila, it's come to my attention that you may have felt a little slighted during last week's announcement. Is that a fair assessment?" Tate smugly asked her in a pitiful failed attempt to empathize.

"No," she calmly stated. "I felt that my exceptional design

talents, intelligence, value and worth to this company were overlooked and undervalued, yet again, because of the color of my skin and my gender. In other words, I wasn't born a privileged white male."

Again, Laila let the awkward silence linger.

"Laila, that's not true," Tate stammered as his face began to turn red with embarrassment. "The partners and I want you to know that you are valued and appreciated. That's why I called you in today. We've decided to create another senior partner position and we want to offer it to you."

"Congratulations on making senior partner at the largest and most prestigious firm in the city," Tate proudly stated.

Laila did not respond as he envisioned. Instead, she calmly sat in purposeful silence and watched Tate begin to squirm as she thought about a measured response.

Laila was loyal to her core, but God was teaching her that opportunity didn't necessarily mean obligation. It was a simple choice in front of her, and it was more than okay to choose herself.

After what seemed like minutes, Laila responded to Tate, "Thank you, but that is not going to work for me. However, I appreciate the offer"

Shocked, Tate stammered, "What?!!"

"May I ask why not?"

"Because I am phenomenally black. I deserve better."

Without apology, Laila gracefully rose from the leather chair and proudly strutted out of Tate's office with her dignity, leaving him open-mouthed, wondering what the hell just happened.

What happened was that Laila had found her voice and made Tate see her. At that moment, she remembered who she was, whose she was, and from where she had come. She had chosen to trust God, bet on herself, and trust Him to deliver on His promises.

Once outside, Laila immediately thanked God and phoned Tre from the bench where they had initially gotten to know each other.

"Babe, guess what? I've decided to start my own firm!"

"Following God's prompting, trusting in Him and His grace has led me to this decision. A decision that will no doubt change my world and the lives of at least six others."

"Sunshine, that's great! You know you have my support and I'll do whatever I can to help with projects and direct clients your way," Tre asserted. The smile on his face and the baritone in his voice oozed sex appeal over the phone.

"Not to worry, babe. God's got it. I'm about to be blessed with two mega clients who believe in me and are willing to back me."

With a smile on her face and a song in her head, Laila hung up the phone and confidently walked two blocks down the street and around the corner to sign the lease on the office where she would hang her own shingle—Allen and Associates.

## ABOUT ANDREA

Andrea is a marketing and business strategist who has empowered and inspired entrepreneurs, small businesses and nonprofits to make their mark and stand out by being their authentic selves. In 2015, Andrea started A Signature Group to give life to her own personal brand and leave an indelible signature mark on the world to inspire and touch people in a meaningful way with what she creates. Andrea is also a contributing co-author of *Behind Her Brand: The Expert Edition* and a guest writer for *Loving on Me* website where she shares her authentic signature experiences, inspiration and faith.

## ACKNOWLEDGEMENTS

Glory to God for planting this story within me. Thanks to my friend Shakenna for inviting me to join this gifted group of writers who fueled and inspired the creative notes of my voice to dance across the pages once again. Blessings and love to our readers!

# story four

# UNWANTED

## LIN O'NEILL

*W*hen did I know? Early on, I think. My dad was overseas when I was born. My mother was living at home with her mother, and their relationship was never good. I was a breech birth, clothed in pain. My mother always said I tried to kill her by being born this way.

The story is that my mother quit feeding me and I almost died until my grandmother had someone, maybe the midwife who delivered me in my grandmother's house, come and see why I cried so much. I was starving. She didn't want to feed me. It was a sign of things to come.

As I got older, my mother verbalized her distaste for having me as her child. Her name for me was STUPID. "STUPID," she'd say to me, "You are so slow!"

"STUPID, you never do anything right!"

"STUPID, why did you do that?"

"You are always so STUPID!"

And she hit me with anything nearby. One time, she hit me with the metal end of a rat-tail comb. The scar is still visible on my forehead at my hairline. Then there was the time she hit me with the hot iron from the ironing board. I was burned and had to have stitches to close the wound. She warned me, "STUPID! Never tell anyone about this or you will be so sorry!"

Those were my first experiences with being touched by her, and it followed me like a gruesome shadow for years. I came of age, mimicking my early life by seeking out relationships that were never approving. There are other examples of the painful residue from my childhood. For example, even today, getting into bed, if the covers are too tight, I can become frantic. That long-ago memory of being held down with a pillow over my face resurfaces and reinforces my need to always be able to move. That is just in case I need to run.

When I was locked in the dark closet for hours on end, there was no one to help.

When I was dropped off at school on the day of a class-mate's birthday celebration, with no present to offer because my mother said she wouldn't get anything for me to share, no one was there to help. For a desperate five-year-old, I tied a bow around an old comic book and put it in the pile of gifts. Someone threw it away, so at least I wasn't embarrassed in front of the others.

My dad never spoke about it. Oddly, similar to the silence he demonstrated to me throughout my life, his last will and testament spoke for him. He wrote, in his rangy, spread-out handwriting, "No need to leave anything for Linda. She's always able to take care of herself." To which I've often thought, "No, Dad, I wasn't." I also thought, "I needed you. You weren't there. All you ever did was emphasize the fact that I was a burden to you too, and that you didn't have time for me in your life of newfound freedom after the divorce.

I worked my way through college, taking 18 hours each semester and holding down two-to-three jobs just to make it. My family's contribution to my education during that first year was seven dollars a week. After that, it was up to me. I was what they called a first-generation student and eventually became the first in my family to graduate from college. My dad and stepmother said they didn't have time for the five-hour drive. Plus, it was too expensive to come to Dallas for my graduation. During what should have been a celebratory time, I was alone again and needing too much.

Surprisingly, my mother somehow found out about my graduation and drove to Dallas. She showed up at my apartment unannounced. I was wearing a beautiful silk blouse that I had bought specifically for the occasion. However, my mother did not share my enthusiasm for the blouse. I remember the moment she said, with every syllable oozing her disapproval, "Why are you wearing something like that?" She yanked on the front of my beautiful blouse so hard it ripped and the buttons flew all over the room. She decided not to attend the ceremony. And on my special day, I proceeded alone, wearing nothing special.

My brother Jeff, who was adored by my dad and given so much approval, had countless opportunities. His college education was paid for from my father's savings, but Jeff never attended. Three weeks before his high school graduation, he dropped out and hitchhiked to California. The police called me early one morning, saying they had put him in jail after picking him up on the Redondo Beach Pier for loitering.

My husband, Frank, went to pick him up. He stayed with us until Frank figured out that he was taking prescription medication from his trainer's bag. Frank was a sports trainer who helped athletes through their injuries. After a few instances of reaching for Seconal and finding his supply diminished, he figured out that Jeff had taken them for himself or to sell. We were never able to figure out which one was which. Yet, I had figured out that when it came to Jeff, he was given what I worked hard to achieve and squandered opportunity, while my efforts to prove my worthiness went unacknowledged and uncelebrated.

The scars have never totally gone away. There has been a lot of therapy, a lot of tears, and an ache that I thought would last forever. My desperate need for affection must have been like a flashing neon sign across my forehead. A sign that only attracted molesters, three of whom took advantage of me when I was very young and were replaced by men who were physically abusive once I grew older. These predatory men and their angry touches, I figured out later, actually filled a need. I might as well have screamed, "Touch me, please! In any way, just touch me, please!"

Years ago, when my mother started sleeping with the alcoholic guy who lived next door, I slept with a butcher knife under my pillow when he spent the night. He scared me; yet, when he flirted with me, somewhere deep inside, I was pleased by the attention. Someone noticed me.

Actually, there was someone who noticed me, or should I say, was dependent on me – Jeff. I basically raised him. I had a routine where I would ride my bike to two stores and pull glass Coke bottles out of the trash to cash them in for the deposit return money. With that money, I would buy baby food and later cans of tuna for Jeff and me. We never had food in the house, and my mother was home only three nights that year. There were no Huggies, so Jeff's cloth diapers had to be washed. I used the old wringer washing machine in the garage. My hands turned blue in the winter cold as I ran those diapers through the wringer, hoping my freezing fingers would not get caught and smashed between the two rollers. I was a ten-year-old substitute mom with no idea of what she was doing.

I responded to this life by becoming a rebel of sorts, if it could be considered rebellious to lie about one's age to secure a job. That's what I did to start working at thirteen at the neighborhood drug store. I worked at the soda fountain until I was fired. It was my first time being fired. The manager said I was hurting his profits because I put too much whipped cream on the fountain orders. I did not really understand, but I sucked it up and found another job. I just figured I was too stupid to hold onto that one.

The cycle finally stopped when I was fifty-five. I carried all this pain for fifty-five years until I said out loud to no one in particular but to the world in general, "No MORE!" In resigning from my old life, I decided to look for the other side of the story I had forgotten. I slowly began to remember one bleak experience after another. It was like an old, cracked black and white movie in the theatre, maybe from World War II. Although it was cold and devoid of feeling, I went through the vault of my memories.

Then, just like the introduction of Technicolor, there she was, my grandmother, a colorful kaleidoscope of hope amid the dreary grey of my memories. She is my angel. I remember that she never called me by anything but my name, even when I made a huge mistake. Like when I let the calf run away with the rope around its neck. I was sure it would catch on a tree branch and be strangled. But instead of calling me stupid like my mother would have, Grandmother just hugged me close, dried my tears and said, "Let's go find that calf."

She kept a quilting frame set up in the front room of the old farmhouse that, even today, I always drive by when I am in town. Once, she tried to teach me to quilt, but I was so afraid I would make a mistake that I quickly did just that. Grandmother said, "We'll find something you like to do much more." That turned out to be making chocolate chip cookies. Looking back, I know how far she had to stretch the money she made from selling eggs and butter to buy the supplies I excitedly used to make those cookies. Yet, being my sweet and wonderful grandmother, she never mentioned the cost.

I also remember the hot summer night, devoid of even a sporadic breeze, when I woke up crying. My parents had announced they were divorcing and Jeff and I had been sent to Grandmother's farm for the summer while they divided the few things they owned. That stiflingly humid night, I awakened from a pillow soaked with tears. Grandmother somehow reached through my sadness, wrapped me into her arms, began softly rocking and intermittently singing old Baptist hymns and telling me everything would be okay.

For years, I must have been the Patron Saint of Repeating Behavior. I always fell for men whose actions and behaviors resembled those of my mother and father. The man I chose to marry was funny and talented, but just not into commitment. We were together for five years before physical abuse literally pushed me back to my familiar. The marriage brought my grandmother's many lessons back to me. Let me tell you the story:

*My grandfather and my biological grandmother had four boys. She died shortly after the birth of the last one. It was the middle of the depression. There were food lines. He was a carpenter. There wasn't any work. He had four hungry little boys to feed, so he married the local spinster.*

That spinster was the incredible woman who would become my grandmother. Of all the lessons she taught me, the one that is most intertwined with my heart's memory of her is the first time I watched her welcome her four stepsons during the family get-together. She and my grandfather added four additional children, with one dying shortly after birth, to their original brood. I vividly remember watching her hug each one of her seven children, showing no difference in her affection, her demeanor, her welcome, or her love between those she inherited and those she birthed.

In my marriage, I was able to honor her by loving beyond measure the four children born to my husband and his first wife. I had learned from my grandmother that all children need love to flourish, and I wanted that for those four amazing children.

My grandmother also taught me, although I didn't realize it at the time, how to be a grandparent. Because of her, I believe grandparents are synonymous with love. Years later, when my children - I call them that because I despise the term "stepchildren"- were old enough to come and spend time with me in the old cabin where I lived in California's Big Sur Mountains, I spent every day replicating what she had done with and for me as an otherwise unloved and scared child. In doing so, my cabin transformed into my version of Grandmother's old farmhouse, where I actually learned how to be what a grandparent is meant to be.

My children and I walked down the hill to the mailbox. We did the chores and fed the animals. We went to town for snacks and played board games just like my grandmother and I did all those years ago. Memories of being a grandmother are almost as warm as those moments with my grandmother when I would fall asleep with my head on her lap as she worked on her latest quilt or read from the worn Bible she kept nearby.

Sometimes when I wonder how I survived, I realize that the answer is actually simple. It was one woman's love for me. Her belief that I was not a mistake, that I had value, and that I could find happiness is what carried me through the darkness. I will remember that forever. She gave me the greatest gift in the world. She gave me the gift of hope.

My grandmother has been gone for a while now. Yet, there still isn't a day I don't feel she is with me. Sometimes motivational speakers talk about "The Power of One." It's true.

Without her being one with me and without the life lessons she modeled, my life would have been devoid of joy and every cell of my body would have withered in the cold darkness of my parents' neglect. I love her today as I did when I was a small child and she walked around in the Texas summer heat letting me do my favorite thing-riding the farm horse, Nelly, up and down, up and down, over and over, again. So many times, we covered the expanse of ground that fronted the farmhouse that I loved.

I love her today as I did when she let me help pull the buckets of water up from the well, letting me believe I was actually doing my share. An encouraging thoughtfulness she repeated when she let me help with the laundry, swirling clothes around in the water with a large wooden paddle in the big black cauldron, water heated over a roaring fire. Back then, I really thought I was helping, but I now know that she was helping me.

I love her today the same way I did when she asked, "Do you want to turn the handle on the ice cream maker?" That was the job usually reserved for the older, stronger kids, but she often let me do it instead.

I love her today as much as I did when we walked through the patch of watermelons and she said, "You get to pick the one for tonight."

I love her today just as I did when she tested the water in the metal #5 washtub for my Saturday bath, making sure it wasn't too hot or too cold but just right.

I love her today as I did when I was a small child and she showed me how to shuck peas. We would sit together in rocking chairs on the front porch, waving at passengers in the occasional car that would pass by. The afternoon would slip away as we prepared a fresh-from-the-garden meal that would be served with dinner. Later, she would pick me up so I could see the array of desserts spread out in the old pie safe that took up a whole wall of the screened-in back porch.

I love her today just as I did when she made sure the huge red-and-black rooster who dominated the backyard and all the hens didn't chase me.

I love her just as I did when she took over churning from me when my arm hurt from the repetitive task that produced the butter she would sell in town that Saturday. I love her just as I did when we would go to church at the tiny building in the woods. She always made sure to carry a fan for each of us to ensure we were comfortable in that oven-hot country sanctuary.

From my grandmother, I learned I was loved. And I love her today exactly the same as I loved her the last time I saw her and kissed her forehead before she died. She was in such pain, but the love she had always shown me was still evident in her touch and in her eyes. I will carry that memory in my heart forever. From my grandmother, I learned that somebody cared for me and loved me beyond what I could see and what I had ever known. Because of my grandmother, I now know I was wanted.

## ABOUT LIN

Lin O'Neill is a Thought Leader, Consultant, Speaker and Facilitator. Lead Faculty for the Goldman Sachs 10,000 Small Businesses Program and Instructor for the SBA's Emerging Leaders Program, Lin has a B.S. in Sociology, M.B.A., is licensed as an Assisted Living Administrator with additional designations of CDP, CMDCP and CADDCT.

Lin's excerpt, *Unwanted*, will resonate with those who grew up in violent and uncaring living situations. It is a testimony to the fact that it only takes one person to right the wrongs of a child's experience. To book Lin O'Neill as a speaker or facilitator, contact lin@oneill.enterprises or lin@alm-ct.com

## ACKNOWLEDGEMENTS

I lovingly dedicate this book to my Grandmother, Irma Husband Jones. And with love to my "Family of Choice": Sharon Smith, Shakenna Williams, Patricia Dameron, Karen Rogers, Debbie Mrazek, Susan Younger, Franca Gargiulo, Elaine Hunt, John Lochner, Art Rousseau and Tanya Daugherty.

And Special Thanks to the Unstuck Writers' Group.

# story five

# RACHEL

## KERRI-ANN PRADERE-JOHNSON

$\mathcal{M}$y Mum used to say, "Rachel, your eyes are so big, bright, and black. The middle reminds me of an ackee's seed growing big and beautiful on the island." When she said this, she usually had my face between her palms, her face close to mine, and a warm smile on her face.Even now, when I think of it, I go on my way with a smile on my face and a skip in my step.

It is Tuesday, and autumn is closing in. The evenings are getting colder, and dusk comes a bit earlier each day. My mother and I finished eating dinner, and it was time to go to my violin class.

In the beginning, mother had to get things like a chart for my feet to stand on, flashcards with musical notes, and paddings that are small and round, like make-up pads, to build a bridge for my violin, my music book, and a rented violin.

For Thanksgiving, Mum's Caribbean roots were on full display as she cooked up a storm! She made curried goat, baked chicken, rice and peas, and more. I laugh now whenever I think that the peas were really kidney beans. Yet, rice and kidney beans do not sound appetizing. Music was playing non-stop, with one song being played numerous times. The UB40's "Cherry Oh Baby" with its skipping introduction, interwoven with another instrument's beat, was the theme song for gatherings. Our singing along and dancing would only pause when I heard a knock on the door. I knew it would be my mother's brother and his family who would visit every Thanksgiving, bringing arm-loads of food. I would help them set it down while really checking for my favorite dish, my aunt's pudding. Later, with bellies full and spirits cheerful, my cousin Kim and I played in my room while the adults all sat, chatted, and ate snacks.

Although the big Christmas church production occurs every year, this particular year would be different as I would be making my début. Kim and I bubbled over with excitement, imagining how well I would do in the production. Between Thanksgiving and Christmas Sunday, they would be practicing the music for each age group's skit. Groups of all ages were given activities to do, and I decided to play "Oh Holy Night" on my violin.

The big night came. It was my time on stage, and I faced the room full of people. I took a deep breath, lifted the violin, and placed it on my collarbone. The violin rested on the ground in between my thumb and index finger. I picked up my bow off of a stool next to me. Positioning my thumb first with the rest of my fingers over the ending of the bow lightly, I followed with my nose looking towards the end of it.

Imagine the sun rising over the horizon, bringing the warmth and brightness of a new day. That's what playing the violin did for me. However, that night, the violin slipped a little from my chin and I played an off-key note. My Mum had taught me how to regain focus and I quickly recovered and very gently shifted the violin back into place as I carried on playing as if nothing had happened. A voice within me said, "Good job!" and the crowd stood to their feet cheering.

I bowed and walked off stage. While descending the stairs, another girl was ascending toward the stage. Her name was Rudi, and her eyes were smaller than mine. As she passed, she said, "I noticed you played a wrong note." I could feel the feeling of happiness starting to sink away and the warm sunrises from the violin turned into sunsets. Soon, I gave up the violin and switched to the keyboard, occasionally playing at our church.

But the warm sunrises did not totally disappear, they would re-emerge when my cousin Kim visited which was usually during holiday breaks and special occasions such as birthdays. My tenth birthday fell on the weekend preceding my start in middle school. I remember it clearly. It was a cool early Saturday morning when I heard the blowing of a car horn by the front of the house, announcing Kim's arrival. Once Mum left the house to do some planting, I went to her room and grabbed two pairs of her shoes (one pink, the other red), two pairs of scarves (one blue and one purple), and two pairs of sun hats. When Mum went to bed, Kim and I pretended we were walking down the runway of a fashion show. Afterward, we stayed up late giggling and catching up with each other, giving updates on what was happening in our lives—not that anything much was happening at that time.

The excitement I had about starting middle school evaporated when I ran into Rudi. When I saw her, I thought, "Is this the same Rudi who had mocked me playing the violin when I was eight years old?" I wondered, "Why did she have to come live with her aunt and uncle in this small town and attend my school anyway?"

One evening, after I finished washing dishes, I was sitting on my bed when I heard the *ring ding-a-ling-a-ling* of our phone, filling our small house. I heard Mum saying, "Rachel, it's for you. Your cousin Kim is on the line. " When I came out of the room, I could see Mum standing there with the phone in her left hand and her other hand on her hip. She looked lazily at me and slowly rolled her eyes at the same time. In taking the phone, I said, "Thanks Mummy," then, "Hey Kim, how yuh doing?" She replied, "I was feeling down today." "Do you know why you felt down?" I asked her." "For no particular reason," she said matter-of-factly. I then changed the subject and asked her, "Do you remember that girl, Rudi, from the Christmas production? Well, guess what? She's now at my new school." Kim's voice escalated to a high-pitched, squealing, "You say what?!" "Just calm down," I said to her. "I know at some point I will have to forgive her." "True," Kim agreed.

I could hear Mummy calling me "Rachel..."

One thing all the girls at school, including Rudi, could agree upon was our admiration for the well-dressed, wonderfully fragrant, good-looking boy named Rich. Once, he and one of his friends came to my home. The friend was talking with me and eventually asked me out. I said, "No" with ease. A month or two after, at a church youth meeting, Rich started a conversation with me and asked, "Do you remember when I came to your house and my friend was trying to ask you out?" I nodded, remembering the time. Rich continued, "I was laughing hearing you come up with all those excuses you gave him." I was thinking, "I didn't know you were listening to the conversation." Then he asked, "If I were to ask you out, would you go out with me?" Without hesitation, I replied, "No, I wouldn't." Confused by my response, he asked, "Why not?" I looked at him seriously and said, "Because all the girls seem to like you, and I do not want to be involved with you like that." He then had the nerve to ask, "If it wasn't for that, would you go out with me?" My response was "No, Rich," and I turned away, leaving him standing there.

The next time Kim visited, she burst into the house, dropped her bag on the floor, and asked, "Auntie, where is Rachel?" I was in the kitchen when I heard her voice. I dried my hands on the towel and went around the corner to greet her. After we hugged, I whispered, "I have something to tell you," and we hurried up the stairs. As soon as I closed the door to my room, words started tumbling out of my mouth, "Rich-the guy all the girls seem to be falling for." Kim asked excitedly, "What is he like?" I said, "Well, I think he fancies me, but I am not sure. This little voice inside me says not to trust Rich." Without hesitating, Kim replied, "Oh well, girl, if that voice is telling you not to trust him, then don't!"

Kim and the little voice inside me were right. Shortly thereafter, I learned that Rich was seeing someone else. But that did not stop him from asking me the same question again. My response was brief and curt: "Aren't you seeing someone else?" To which he responded coldy, "No, we broke up." While attempting to hide his surprise that I knew, I walked away, leaving him there with his mouth open.

When I started playing the keyboard at church, the church began to grow. I would like to think it was because of my keyboard playing, but honestly, it was because of Pastor Lee and his wife, Pam. They were a big part of the community, especially Pam, with her friendliness and constant encouragement. She was a people magnet, while the pastor maintained relationships with the original members, especially my family. Together, they grew the church.

Years passed and I played the piano during worship for eleven of them on a Sunday per rota. I had also started working with a youth program at the YMCA, Monday through Friday, with Sundays off and some odd Saturdays here and there. During my time working for the church, the voice that told me to turn down Rich would talk to me more frequently. The voice would often point out lessons from my childhood, like "I kept you safe by climbing over the fence to pick fruits." Actually, the voice had been there through elementary, middle, and upper high school, guiding me through those years with Rudi.

It's funny how some people and some feelings from the past continue to reappear even after you have walked away from them, like Rich. During the eleven years, to try and win my affection, Rich often reminded me of Rudi's ugly comment about my favorite dress. "Is that the only dress she has?" My feelings were hurt by the comment and that he would choose to tell me that. Yet, I heard the gentle voice inside me say, "*You are loved. You are the apple of my eye, and you are a diamond too.*" And yes, I heard the gentle voice, but when I really thought about Rudi's comments, I couldn't help but ask why. I wondered if she said those mean things because I was considered fair-skinned. I wished I could put aside those thoughts for another day. Some may ask why couldn't I put aside those thoughts, and I would tell them that's not how I was raised.

We were approaching the annual milestone of the twelfth anniversary of the big Christmas production. I was no longer the little girl who missed a note on the violin. I was one of the organizers. After arriving for the first rehearsal, I walked through the mini hall to the back room and made my way up to the main sanctuary where all the other bodies were to start practice. Some of us were early, but there was still time for small talk.

Ms. Lue, who oversaw the production, handed me some

papers and said, "Please go and give Pastor Lee these papers for me." I retraced my steps back to that mini hallway where the stairs led up to Pastor Lee's office. As I approached the office, I could hear some voices coming from behind the door. One voice was asking, "How are we going to handle the numbers for this production?" I knocked and waited for an answer. "Come on in," the voice instructed. I did and gently pushed the door open. Immediately, I recognized the two pastors from the area, but there was a third person who I had never seen before. I delivered the papers and went back in time for practice. In no time, I finished and was back at home.

The following practice, Ms. Lue again requested that I take some papers to Pastor Lee. This time, after I knocked and pushed the door open, there was a young man who I did not recognize with Pastor Lee. He was sitting with his arms resting on the frame of the chair. His feet were flat on the floor, with his body pressed back into the chair in a relaxed fashion. "Rachel, this is Thomas Junior," Pastor Lee said casually when he saw me.

His eyes were small and sat squarely in his round face which was framed by his small afro that seemed bushy and plentiful. His skin was beautiful without any blemish and his demeanor was confident but not cocky. Thomas, Jr., who was also known as Michael, lived with both parents, Mr. and Mrs. Thomas. He did well in school and his teachers considered him bright, but he could get bored easily. His parents sought to address his boredom with strictness and piano lessons. His experience with the piano would be one of the reasons we connected so easily.

During a Saturday night rehearsal for the upcoming Christmas program, Pastor Lee made two important announcements. The first was that the Christmas program would become a part of the New Year's Celebration events. The second was introducing Michael to the number of members who were on hand that night. He then called Michael to the podium to say a few words. When Michael spoke, his baritone captivated my attention. I think he thanked the pastor and introduced his partner who would help with the production. I'm not really sure because I was floating on the melody of his tone of voice.

Shortly after rehearsal, Michael approached me and said, "Hi, I'm Mike, short for Michael." I looked up at him and both of us began to smile. I replied, "Yes, and don't we all know." We shared a laugh before he said, "Okay, you know my name. I heard your name is Rachel. It's a pretty name." I suppose the combination of him knowing my name and his saying it in that tantalizing voice made me think, "Is he my knight in shining armor?" I looked back up at him, but I did not know what to say other than, "I guess I will see you at the next practice."

At the next practice, things became a bit more demanding. A few choir members quit after becoming frustrated with the vocal arrangements. I was exhausted from having to play with the choir and the other program events. Yet, I saw Mike, and I got the impression that he was waiting until practice was over so that he could finish talking to me. As I was gathering my things and tidying up to go home, I heard his voice just over my shoulder. "Hello!" I turned around, mildly startled, and he said, "Do you want to have coffee with me?" To which I replied, "I don't think so." Curiously, he asked me, "Why not? I would love to hear it." I picked up my bag and said, "Because I don't think it is a good idea. Plus, I had better be going."

I left. Yet, as I reflected on our exchange, I realized that I did not hear any objection from the voice inside of me. That made me decide to call Kim and tell her about Michael. When I told her, she squealed and giggled, "Is he fine?"

"Yes girl..." I admitted.

"Then go for it!" she encouraged.

So I did. After the next practice, Mike asked me out again. "What about tonight?" he inquired. "There is no excuse." I responded, "Hmmmm." He followed that with, "I won't take no for an answer." To which I feigned thinking it over with my head slightly to the side, carefully looking at him to say, "Okay."

We walked across the church parking lot to the café house. Once inside, there was an empty sofa and chair by the window, seeming to beckon us over. After getting comfortable and placing our orders, we looked into each other's eyes and then quickly away almost like school kids. Mike broke through our bashfulness and asked, "Other than playing the keyboard, what else do you do?" I said, "I work at the YMCA with young people." I paused before adding, "I suppose you work with churches, Michael?" "Yes, I work with churches on their programming systems, computers, and stuff like that," he replied. Then the waitress brought our sandwiches and hot drinks. We sat and ate in silence for a moment before Mike started talking about his upbringing and how he played the piano too. I began talking about my family, and before we knew it, it was nightfall and time for us to leave.

There is a level of excitement that comes with New Year's Day that was amplified throughout our community in anticipation of the production. In fact, people were lined up with their passes to get inside for the show. Those of us in the show were backstage getting ourselves prepared. Pam and Ms. Lue, along with the rest of the team, were busy making sure we were all ready. The show began with a prayer, a selection from the choir, and a solo, followed by a play about the Prodigal Son. The grand finale was a sermon by Pastor Lee taken from St. John chapter 3 verse 16.

After a full night of piano duties, I needed some fresh air, so I went outside for a breather. A few minutes later, Mike came out to join me. He cleared his throat and said, "It is a bit chilly out here." My response was "Yes, it is..." and before I could say anything else, he offered his jacket to me. "Take it." I appreciatively slipped my arm into the sleeves and thanked him for his courtesy. He responded by leaning over and asking, "Would you go out on an evening date with me a week from this Saturday?" As I rose to my feet, I moved closer to him, saying, "Yes," and sharing a smile before stepping off to go back inside. I looked up and saw two ladies coming out of the building behind him. I noticed one had a spring in her stride and the other was hopping.

When I returned to the sanctuary, the pastors were praying for those who wanted prayer, and I made my way toward the front of the church. As Pastor Lee was praying, I had an epiphany of sorts. I had a glimpse of me playing the piano along with a younger me playing the violin flash before my eyes. I shared this vision with Mike on our date.

We were seated in a nice restaurant looking through a clear glass window with silver shimmers of moonlight making patterns along the water. Not only was the night beautiful, but Mike was attentive. After pulling out my chair and eventually placing our orders, he stared at me from across the table. With a look of compassion, he asked, "How was your day? "It was fine and yours?" I said.

"Mine was fine too," he replied. "What were your thoughts on the show?"

"It was good, but something puzzled me." I shared. "What did you do?" he asked, with a look of curiosity.

"When I went up for prayer, I saw myself playing the piano and then the violin on stage in front of a huge audience. It was confusing. I am not sure what all of that was about?"

At that moment, something distracted me. First, I heard her voice, and then I saw her face. I looked closer as I focused my gaze on her familiar eyes. Rudi was standing there looking at me and saying to her friend, "That was the girl who could not play the violin."

Gently, Mike said, "Don't pay her any mind. Have you ever

considered that maybe she was and is obviously still jealous of you?"

Perplexed, I responded, "Hmm, I never thought about that."

He asked, "So, you did play the violin at one point?" I nodded my head yes while still accepting how Rudi's jealously had stung me that first night and was a nuisance throughout middle school. I refocused on Mike when he asked, "Did you stop because of her?"

I nodded my head, "yes" again.

"If that is the case, then perhaps you should start playing again."

It was right then that he leaned into me and gently kissed me. As I felt my heart float away, he gently and slowly pulled back and said, "Now what about us?" Immediately, I looked up and Rudi was still there, standing with her back turned. As usual, Rudi was pointing to someone talking so I leaned forwards with my hand on the chair pulling it out. With a squeak from the chair, Rudi turned and looked in my direction. I walked over to where she and her friend were standing and said, "You know what, Rudi? You talk too much." I spun around and walked right back to where Mike and I were sitting so that we could go.

## ABOUT KERRI-ANN

I remember sitting in a café in Delhi, India, reading in a magazine an author's story on what inspired her to write. I left feeling even more inspired. That inspiration lead to my first book, *Love Sees Her* (available on Amazon).

When I heard about this book project, I asked myself, "What am I going to put in the book?" The next day, I woke up with the main storyline. *Rachel*, is a fiction romance in which I have interwoven my faith with additional interesting storylines. I hope you enjoyed reading it.

## ACKNOWLEDGEMENTS

To my great-aunt Annette McIntosh Pascal, I trust this will make you even more proud of my endeavors and achievements.

This story includes a tribute to my sister Felicia (Mother Jennifer McIntosh) and is dedicated to her memory.

# story six

# UNDERGROUND HOPE

## VIRGINIA LEE FORTUNATO

"Ahhhh," Bianca exclaimed after she kicked off her high-heeled, peep-toe pumps, pulled the hair tie from her long, blonde hair and flopped her exhausted body onto the couch. With chopsticks held between her teeth, she flipped open the container of Buddha Garden Chicken Chow Mein and screwed the top off a bottle of San Pellegrino. As she balanced the food on her lap, she carefully reached for the remote and turned on the TV before she positioned her tired feet on the coffee table. The screen immediately glowed and featured a news channel that she had watched previously. She rolled her eyes and hovered her thumb over the remote's guide button, as she was anxious to watch something that would not make her brain hurt. Before she could change channels, she heard the news anchor mention her hometown, Mountain Brook, Alabama. She wondered aloud, "Why is he talking about my hometown on the Atlanta news station?" Bianca became consumed with curiosity, placed the remote aside, deftly worked her chopsticks, and plunged a mound of soy sauce-drenched goodness into her mouth.

. . .

"Today, two men were charged with the murder of twenty-two-year-old Dante Phillips of Birmingham, Alabama. Local racial justice advocates are furious that it has taken seven months to secure arrest warrants for the men who tracked Mr. Phillips to perform a citizen's arrest." After turning the volume down, Bianca snatched her phone, opened the search engine, and typed, "Dante Phillips Alabama death" and shouted, "How did I miss this?"

She clicked on the first report and began to process the details. Dante Phillips was seen leaving a Mountain Brook home. He checked the door of a truck in the driveway and walked toward the street. The Hudson brothers, who lived across the street, witnessed Mr. Phillips' pulling on the handle of the work truck and, because they were on high alert after a series of recent car break-ins, jumped in their own truck and drove up to Mr. Phillips who was walking down the street. The brothers retreated from their vehicle and one pointed a rifle in Mr. Phillips' face. Mr. Phillips fled while the other brother yelled after him, "Stop, stop, stop! You're under arrest!" The brothers got back into their vehicle and sped down the hill as Mr. Phillips tripped and fell to the ground. This time, a brother jumped from the rolling vehicle and again pointed a gun at Mr. Phillips, who pushed the weapon away and attempted to get up before being fatally shot twice in the chest.

Bianca stared open-mouthed at her cell phone as she scrolled through images of a crime scene in a neighborhood that looked all too familiar. She continued talking to herself, "How did the news have all of these details?"

Bianca clicked on the first link in the search engine list, a follow-up to the seven-month-old news story with an update added just two days prior. "Hudson Brothers Conviction Secured After New Video Footage Uncovered". A homeowner, Cecily Edenborrow, in the neighborhood where the crime was committed, told police she didn't have video footage of the murder. Later, bragging to her friends, Cecily admitted she got the actual shooting on video and one of the friends posted the video to YouTube. Bianca, who was friends with Cecily on social media, began scrolling through Cecily's social media posts about the recently revealed video footage. First, she saw Cecily's take on the clip—"I stand by my decision to withhold the video from the police. I've known Paul and Jeff for two decades as neighbors and friends, and I am confident the brothers are good Christian men, who would never shoot anyone without just cause." Next, Bianca scrolled through comments from other neighbors and Mountain Brook community members who were supportive of Cecily's decision to withhold evidence. Reading comment after comment, Bianca sensed that beneath the bluster and outrage, the common emotion was fear. Each person showed up to Cecily's social media page as an individual and left as a member of a collective group, unified in their fear. A group that had picked a side, a side declaring that the Hudson brothers were justified in their actions to hunt down and shoot Dante Phillips.

The more Bianca read the comments, the more she witnessed fear escalating the group's collective anger. As an outsider looking in, Bianca felt like this was holding marionette puppet strings attached to the social media followers' emotions. Someone would post a new perspective on their collective fear and it would explode into a series of comments validating and communicating their fear through anger. The collective supporters of the Hudson Brothers articulated the driving force behind these intense emotions through their comments defending Cecily's decision not to reveal the footage to the police. Their overarching fear was that the media would manipulate the footage and turn it into something the community believed it was not. The community feared the shooting of a black man by a white man would become a racially charged incident. However, from their perspective, the Hudson brothers were simply protecting their neighborhood. With that belief, the social media mob felt it was their responsibility to protect the brothers and felt justified doing so, even if their behavior was illegal, like in Cecily's withholding of evidence.

After reading the comments on Cecily's social media page for thirty minutes, Bianca clicked over to YouTube to watch the security camera footage of the Hudson brothers shooting Dante. Based on the news reports, Bianca knew the incident occurred several months back, but she didn't know the exact date. Pressing play on the video, she immediately saw the date at the bottom of the camera footage--*January 2nd*. "Wait!" was the alarming thought in her head, "I was home on January 2nd!" Before she even had a chance to watch Dante's murder, a barrage of images replayed in her head.

Like a tidal wave of truth, Bianca faced the reality of what she had witnessed while driving through her parents' neighborhood that fateful day. At least ten cop cars careened en masse as their blue lights reflected off the white and grey siding of the suburban homes. The cars were surrounded by a white, standard, body-sized sheet, laid flat across the asphalt. The white sheet would not be removed until a body bag was brought to the scene and the victim's body was zipped inside it. Bianca was then struck with a thunderbolt of realization, "Dante was under the white sheet!!!" She drew in her breath, fell back onto the couch cushions, and spilled food all over the floor. She didn't care about the mess. She was shocked as her mind flashed back to the moments she had not considered one time in the last seven months.

Bianca stayed with her parents in Mountain Brook over New Year's Eve, and although she planned to head back to Atlanta on January 1st, her hangover didn't allow her to leave until the following evening, January 2nd. As the sun began to sink below the horizon, she drove towards the neighborhood's exit and witnessed the police cars parked along the roadside of the suburbia neighborhood. A uniformed police officer used hand motions to help her veer her car safely through the crime scene which encompassed a body beneath a white sheet. Bianca saw a black woman nearby, with her head stooped low, who was comforted by a man kneeling next to her. Bianca remembered an immediate jumbled mess of thoughts that scrambled through her mind as she drove by the crime scene.

"Oh my gosh! Someone died."

"That's unusual to see a black couple in this neighborhood."

"Poor lady! She obviously cared for the person under the sheet."

"Why are they still on the side of the road?"

"Mimi would have stopped to support them."

Mimi, her beloved grandmother, was such a supporter of the black community and would have stopped to ask more questions. Remembering her, Bianca began to apply the brake and ease her car towards the curb. *BB-RRING... BB-RRING ... BB-RRING.* "Dammit!" she exclaimed as the piercing cell phone ringtone blared over the speakers.

Following the New Year's Party, she had left the volume up way too loud and the disorienting rings blared through the speakers, which aggravated her lingering headache. She saw the name of her domineering boss on her SUV's navigation screen and realized it was his fifth call of the day. She knew she'd told her boss she'd leave Alabama and get back to Atlanta that morning, but hadn't had the wherewithal to get out of bed any earlier than the time the clock read which was 5 *pm.* Bianca gazed into the rearview mirror at the hurting couple and felt a twinge of guilt as she hesitated for a moment before deciding to deal with her overbearing boss instead of comforting the hurting couple. Promising herself she would find out later what happened, she veered out onto the highway, clicked the answer button on her cell phone, and between her clenched teeth, attempted to sound as polite as possible as she half-yelled, "Yes Richard! I'm heading back to Atlanta now!"

Because of the rarity of the event, Bianca made a promise to herself to find out more about the crime scene. Between the cop cars, the dead body and the black couple in an overwhelmingly white neighborhood, there was enough irregularity that she knew she wanted to find out more. However, when she returned to Atlanta, she did not keep the promise she'd made to herself. She never heard anything else about the incident from her parents, who lived in the neighborhood, and she did not conduct her own research on why the couple was huddled over the white sheet. Instead, after driving comfortably in her black Lexus SUV along I20-East, her thoughts were consumed with her job and the corporate clients she was paid handsomely to defend. The crime scene faded from her thoughts. Seven months later, she sat in her extravagantly designed living room with an expensive rug covered in Chow Mein and a dazed expression on her face. The shooting happened less than a mile from where she was staying at her parents' house, and she was clueless about its occurrence. She had slept late, hoping to recover from a hangover, oblivious that a black man had literally run for his life, only to be executed by the Hudson brothers.

Sadly, it took tonight's news blaring from her TV for Bianca to even notice that this devastating event had occurred. When was the last time she made a conscious attempt to think about people within the black community? She reflected on her personal social media feed which used to be peppered with people of all shades of black and brown. Years ago, before becoming engrossed in her high-paying corporate lawyer job, she was actively engaged in standing up against racial injustice and had engaged in meaningful connections with those whose lives were impeded by those injustices. Now, that inter-racial community felt so distant from her present circumstances. She had lost the racial connection that was cultivated by her grandmother, Mimi, who spent her entire adult life advocating for racial equality and whom Bianca credited more for rearing her than her own mother. From an early age, Bianca possessed a tender spirit that was not consumed with the social norms her mother religiously followed.

During her formative childhood years, Bianca felt more at home with her grandmother, who paid special attention to cultivating her granddaughter's tender spirit. In Mimi's home, the focus was on positively impacting the world outside her home, instead of focusing on following social norms within. She spent as much time as possible at her grandmother's home, located two miles away from her parents' residence. Bianca would often head out to the bus line after school and take a hard right towards the front of the line where the yellow bus to her grandmother's neighborhood stood waiting. At least once a week, Ms. Diane, the bus driver on the route to her grandmother's neighborhood, would stare into the blue eyes of the school-aged girl and tell her that there was no more room on this bus. With a twinkle in her eye, she would glance over her shoulder, then look back to young Bianca and change her mind, "Well, maybe just this one time I can fit you in." Ms. Diane knew as well as the other bus driver and teachers, that Bianca's mother, as well-intentioned as she was, had more passion for showing up to a PTA meeting carrying a perfectly laid out tray of deviled eggs than she did for the actual hands-on parenting required to rear a little girl well.

Bianca learned very early on that her mother was not going to provide the kind of mothering she craved, and this pushed her straight into her grandmother's open arms. Her grandmother, Bianca "Mimi" Marie Fanning, was a white woman who used her privilege to stand up for her black brothers and sisters and expose her granddaughter to a side of American life that went unnoticed in her parents' home. Her mother's home was dusted, vacuumed, and polished, like a perfectly made-up doll, beautiful on the outside with little substance on the inside. There was never any room for a child's muddy shoes, a book bag full of school projects, or an overactive creative imagination that may have disrupted the order of the home. Obsessed with their home and the people invited into it, Bianca's mother spent most days full of social outings that included the bridge club, book club, and lunch at the club. The outings kept her busy and left Bianca free to choose where she wanted to spend her days. She chose to spend most of them with Mimi.

Sometimes the pair of grandmother and granddaughter would sit at the red lacquered kitchen table to work on homework, and the older would tell the younger what a privilege it was to get an education. Sometimes they would sit on the back deck with their feet propped up in the sunshine, and the younger would tell the older about the latest trends discussed at school. On other days, they would make signs in preparation for a weekend protest after another black life was extinguished for an unjust reason. Mimi would always share stories from her past and examples of the continued realities of racial injustice in the present. Between the walls of a pale blue townhouse, Bianca found comfort and purpose for her life, woven together through the endless hours spent with Mimi.

Wishing Mimi was still a phone call away, Bianca snapped back to the present and continued to scroll through search results, observing all the work the racial justice community had done on behalf of Dante Phillips. It was the stuff her grandmother would have been a part of, not only as a participant but as a frontline advocate and leader. Mimi would have organized protests, gathered petition signatures, participated in sit-ins, and written letters to law enforcement and government officials. Those advocating for justice for Dante Phillips had been working for months to try to get those in charge to pay closer attention to the man's death, and Bianca had been unaware of all of it.

She raised her eyes from the phone screen and came face-to-face with a picture of her grandmother, taken during the Poor People's March in 1968, holding a "Marching for Freedom" sign. The black and white, fuzzy printed, tattered-edged photo hung over the TV cabinet, next to a perfectly posed, perfectly touched up, brightly colored, matching outfit family photo of her and her parents. Looking into the black and white photo of Mimi's determined face, Bianca recalled how her beloved grandmother quoted Rosa Parks:

> *"People always say that I didn't give up my seat*
> *because I was tired, but that isn't true...*
> *No, the only tired I was was tired of giving in."*

Bianca burst into tears. "Mimi, I've failed you. Where did I go wrong? When did I put my torch down? What made me give in?"

Ten years ago, Bianca would have been arm-in-arm with her Freedom Rider grandmother, marching on the front lines of the protests, motivating people to sign petitions, sending and writing letters, and advocating relentlessly for Dante's murderers to be captured. But now, years after Mimi transitioned into heaven, Bianca had lost touch with all her old justice-fighting friends and was in the dark about this battle presently being fought. She looked at the family photo next to the picture of Mimi on the frontlines, a perfect demonstration of the two different worlds Bianca lived in as a young girl. Until Mimi died, Bianca had one foot in each, but realized she'd strayed from Mimi's world and now stood fully planted in a polished one, like her parents' carefully crafted, societal norm-following, way of life.

Feeling disappointed in how far she'd strayed from her

priorities, Bianca wished her precious grandmother could put her arm around her shoulders. As she attempted to replicate Mimi's warmth by pulling a green, macramé blanket across her lap, tears began to trickle down from her cheeks onto the blanket as she nestled into a corner on her leather couch. She purchased that couch with the money she had made as a successful, big corporation defense attorney. A gift to herself after winning her first big case, the couch cost a fortune, but it was the blanket that was the true treasure because the green blanket was the only one her grandmother crocheted while on this side of heaven. Mimi loved the idea of creating art with her hands and would have made more blankets if she'd had the time, but she spent all her days participating in activities that advocated for racial justice.

Once her tears dried, Bianca couldn't sit still any longer. She had to do something. She grabbed her phone and called her mom.

"Hey, sweetie! How are you?"

"Mom, why didn't you tell me about Dante Phillips' death?"

"Wait, honey, who died? Who's Dante?"

"MOM! Back in January, a man was killed in our own neighborhood. How do you know nothing about that?"

"I don't know. I didn't think it was that big of a deal. People around here talked a little bit about it, but mostly it wasn't even covered in the local news. The kid was breaking into houses and cars and stole Ms. Felicity's cell phone out of her front seat. I hate that he died, but he wouldn't have died if he wasn't doing the wrong thing."

Bianca paused, realizing she made the call without a second thought about what she was doing. Bianca's mother, Lanette, was a woman who had no interest in following in Mimi's footsteps. Lanette spent many days home alone after school because her mother was out advocating for racial equality. Mimi would invite her daughter along to participate, but from an early age, Lanette chose to spend her days investing in the friendship that later became her husband and Bianca's father. Spending most of her days at his house, Lanette became a parrot of her future father-in-law's rhetoric; "Slavery was abolished over a hundred years ago; we're all equal under the Constitution and black folks reap what they sow – using drugs and shooting each other and, dammit, that's what they get for having so many babies without fathers." Because of the way she grew up, Bianca and her mother never saw eye-to-eye on topics involving race.

"... Bianca?"

Her mother's voice snapped Bianca back into the present. "Uh... yeah... Sorry, Mom...For a second, I got distracted. I guess it just shocked me that I was at your house the day the murder happened and didn't find out about it until I saw it on the news tonight."

"It made the news in Atlanta?"

"Yeah, apparently the Hudson brothers were arrested tonight for killing Dante."

"Arrested? What?! Honey, I've got to go. I need to call their mother and see if she needs any help rounding up bail money. How ridiculous. Two men were trying to keep my neighborhood safe, and now they are in jail."

*Click!* Bianca's mother hung up the phone.

Bianca sat and stared at the phone but felt a sense of gratitude that her mom had ended the conversation so abruptly. It was a conversation she was all too familiar with having with the woman who gave her life. It was conversation they had had many times previously — a conversation that always ended in an argument because Bianca stood firm in her position that racism was still a problem in America and her mother always denied that it wasn't. Why did she even call her mom about this issue anyway? Was it a momentary lapse of sanity? "Ouch!" Bianca said out loud as that realization engulfed her.

Bianca couldn't remember the last time she'd argued with her mother. It had been years, maybe five or more, since she'd cared enough about racial issues to go head-to-head with her mom. Presently, all their phone calls consisted of local Mountain Brook gossip, travel plans, work challenges, and the constant dialogue of mother-nagging-daughter as to when she was going to get married and provide the family with grandchildren.

Something her mom said triggered emotions tied to a memory of her grandmother, Mimi. In their call, her mother said, "I hate that he died, but he wouldn't have if he wasn't doing the wrong thing." Because of how much time she spent with Mimi before she died, Bianca instinctively sensed that countless black men and women died because people assumed they were up to no good when, in fact, they were entirely innocent. Which was it this time? Was Dante innocent or was her mom right? Was Dante doing something wrong?

If she were honest with herself about where she grew up, Bianca had to admit it was rare for a black man to be in the Mountain Brook neighborhood. Maybe he was breaking into cars and stealing cell phones. Bianca strongly disagreed with the citizen's arrest law, which gave citizens the right to arrest their own neighbors with force. Regardless of her feelings about the outdated law, if Dante was doing something wrong and the Hudson brothers believed they were arresting a guilty man, wouldn't they be within their rights to protect their neighborhood? Question after question rumbled through Bianca's mind with relentlessness. Bianca scrolled through countless news articles desperate for answers. Was Dante doing something wrong? She honestly did not know.

In an answer to her question, Bianca heard the soft, gentle words of her grandmother as audibly as if she were sitting in the room. "Does it matter?"

Many years ago, Mimi answered this question after the

police shooting of a black man named Sean. There were so few facts about the situation that the case was hard to follow. Other officers on the scene were not wearing body cameras yet, so the situation inevitably turned into the typical he said-she said speculation between other officers on the scene and people who witnessed the exchange. As they watched the events reported on the nightly news, Bianca and Mimi looked over their plates of spaghetti to hear the all-too familiar words. "Police showed up after they received a call about a suspicious-looking black male spotted in the local neighborhood," the blonde-haired reporter said, with an unengaged tone in his voice. He reported similar stories almost verbatim so many times in his career that he could do so without the aid of the teleprompter. He then proceeded to say that the police found Sean walking on the side of the road nearby when he was approached because he looked suspicious. Sean took off running, and the police pursued him as their blue lights lit up the night sky and the sound of the high-pitched sirens gave voice to their chase. "What was Sean doing wrong?" Bianca remembered asking Mimi. Mimi answered softly, with a futile tone, "Does it matter?"

Her question was not intended to excuse potential bad behavior if, in fact, the young man being approached by police was doing something wrong, but rather to challenge the situation in its entirety. All too often, the report of a suspicious-looking black man had nothing to do with the actions of the individual in question but rather the emphasis on the color of the person's skin. Bianca, herself, locked her car doors when someone came walking down the road next to her vehicle, and if she was honest with herself, she did this less when it was a white person than a black person. The idea that a person of color is to be regarded with more suspicion than a white person was a belief so deeply ingrained in her unconscious that it was hard to identify without digging. Sure, if someone is doing something wrong or illegal, that person should be reported to the authorities, but how often are the actions of a black person, especially a black man, walking through a neighborhood considered suspicious and therefore wrong? When, in fact, the only thing he's doing is walking down a street. Upon hearing a story like that, Mimi didn't want her granddaughter's first question to be "What was this person doing wrong?" because it assumed the individual was guilty. She wanted, instead, for Bianca to presume innocence first. She wanted her to take a step back and ask a different question, "Was this person actually doing something wrong?"

During that same conversation, to help Bianca understand further where she was coming from, Mimi asked her if she'd ever been in a situation where she was walking down the road and was stopped by the police. In Bianca's eighteen years of life, she couldn't recollect a single time. Then Mimi asked her what she would do and how she would feel if it happened to her. Bianca responded that she would be nervous, but that she would stop and talk to the officers. She wasn't doing anything wrong so she had no reason to run. There was no reason to fear them.

Mimi seized upon the word "fear" with a far-off look in her eye and remembered years of conversations she had had with mothers of black and brown girls and boys. Leveraging these memories, she talked to Bianca about what it was like to be a young black child in America. As Mimi talked, she saw faces of black friends and mothers she marched with on the east coast and the west coast and everywhere in between, who taught their children, especially their sons, how to behave in public and particularly when stopped by police, fearful of the consequences if they didn't. She recounted the instructions from the mothers to their sons:

"Don't wear your hood."

"Don't put your hands in your pockets."

"Don't move suddenly."

"Don't talk back."

"Don't run."

"Put your hands up."

Mimi shared one particular tearful moment she had decades ago with a fellow racial justice-seeking sister as the mother of three black sons confessed through sobs, "I don't know what to do anymore. I don't know how to save them. I don't know how to keep them safe. I just don't know." Bianca began to understand the fear these mothers faced as she was exposed to Mimi's experiences with people she marched alongside for decades. Bianca had no reason to fear the police any more than her mother had reason to teach her how to behave around officers. She'd been lectured her entire life about how to behave in public.

"Cross your legs."

"Sit up straight."

"Put your napkin on your lap."

"Chew with your mouth closed."

"Say 'Yes ma'am' and 'No ma'am.'"

None of the instructions she received from her mom were going to make any difference between life and death. Surely, her mother feared for her safety. What mother doesn't? All moms worry about their kids. But Mimi was exposing and explaining a level of worry Bianca's mom never had to fear for her children.

She snapped back to her present moment in her polished, dominantly white, expertly decorated living room. The news was playing in the background, and Mimi's march photo was staring back at her. Bianca began to stroke the green macramé blanket. Finding comfort in its weave, she longed for those conversations with her grandmother. Mimi was a safe place, a cocoon of comfort. She never judged Bianca's questions. She never criticized her ignorance. She just gave her space to process all her emotions and wade through the things she'd been taught all her life by her parents, her community and the society she lived in. In that cocoon of safety, Bianca was able to wrestle with her own denial and defensiveness about race relations and her place in America. She was able to ask the hard questions with which she grappled and cultivate a listening ear and a teaching spirit to walk her through these events.

Since her grandmother wasn't around to talk with anymore, Bianca realized how little she had allowed herself to think about race or the struggles of her black and brown friends, because quite honestly, she didn't know whom to talk to about what was floating around in her mind. Bianca looked, again, at the picture of her beautiful grandmother and realized how desperately she missed Mimi. She felt hopeless and alone. Without Mimi's voice to guide her, for the first time that night, she realized it was now her turn to figure out how she would confront this moment. Bianca knew the process would get messy and uncomfortable. "Am I ready?" she wondered as her thoughts drifted back to her unanswered question, "Did Dante do something wrong?"

Details! That's what she needed. She found and began reading through a report on the case. Apparently, Dante, whose boss was still on holiday vacation, had answered an early morning maintenance call at a rental property managed by a company that had employed him for four years. Not typically assigned to Mountain Brook properties, Dante traveled from Birmingham to represent his boss with a nasty, clogged toilet situation so the renters would not be inconvenienced any longer. The renters, who didn't have any cars in the driveway because they had flown in and had taken a cab from the airport, had just waved goodbye and thanked Dante at the door. In his early morning haste, Dante walked to his truck only to discover that he'd locked the keys in the cab. He sent a text to his boss and told him he was going to walk to the nearest restaurant to order breakfast before dealing with the key fiasco. That was the last text he would ever send.

*WHAM!* Bianca hurled her phone across the room as it landed face down at the base of the wall opposite the couch. She was mad that Dante died for doing nothing wrong. Mad that the Hudson brothers had chased him down based only on preconceived notions, not actual evidence. Mad her mom never told her about the crime committed in their very own neighborhood. Mad, the community was making efforts to protect the Hudson brothers instead of supporting the Phillips family. Mad! This kind of murder happened again! Mad that it happened under her very own nose and furious at herself for not knowing about it until just seven minutes ago. Bianca was wracked with so many feelings and emotions.

"Mimi, what do I do with all of this?" She cried out in the empty apartment. "You're not here. What do I do with all of this?" Hot, angry tears trickled down her face as she dropped her head down to her thighs. Snot dripped onto Mimi's blanket on her lap as she sobbed while wading through the different stages of grief. She let herself process the weighty emotions of the moment until, with no tears left to cry, she got up from the couch and started pacing the floor. Back and forth, back and forth she sauntered.

Emotions developed in her mind, but she couldn't even identify what they were. "Who could she talk to?" she wondered. She felt utterly alone. Still pacing, she knew she had to do something. "But what?" Needing something to do with her hands and a place to put all those feelings, Bianca walked back to her bedroom to sit in the chair across from her king-sized bed situated next to the window-the place where she read and wrote and thought and meditated and dreamed. One of her favorite places to be, and yet, she hadn't spent time in that favorite place for quite a while. Grabbing her journal, she opened it to the last entry dated April 17th. With her favorite hot pink felt tip pen in hand, she turned the page and wrote the date at the top... *July 6th, 2021.* She paused, unsure of where to start. She closed her eyes, took a deep breath and placed words on paper. The words burst forth, and she couldn't write fast enough. Her brain was firing thoughts faster than the paper could catch them. Seven pages later, she stared back at her truth. Hopelessness rose from the paper and stared her firmly in the eyes.

"I'll never be able to find my way back to Mimi's passion," she sobbed. Mimi's passion. "Oh, my goodness!" she sat upright, shocked by the revelation. This cause was Mimi's passion. "Was it ever really my own?" she asked as reality embedded itself.

Mimi was the one always keeping me in the loop on racial justice issues. She would send me news articles, petitions, and protest dates. It was Mimi who was rejected by her own family for her beliefs, who marched with Dr. King, who stood on the bridge in Selma and narrowly escaped with her life during the Freedom Rides. It was Mimi who suffered for the racial justice cause and allowed me to put a hand on the torch she carried. "Shit!" Bianca fell back in her chair, defeated, ashamed and mulling, "I stood on the back of her legacy, counting on her passion to sustain me for the long haul, and now, with her gone, the passion is gone as well. When she died, I didn't pick up her torch and carry it as my own. I allowed her legacy to die with her, assuming I'd always care about what she cared about since I'd been around it all of my life." There it was...

The truth was sprawled out in front of Bianca in plain sight. She gently laid her pen down on the journal page and permitted her tears to fall. Moist tears trickled down her face as her emotions were given full sway to have their way with her. She had reached a dead end. She had let Mimi down, and her pen now felt heavy and impossible to pick up again while she herself felt incapable of moving forward. Bianca sat frozen, breathing in and out for some time. Her eyes remained glued to the page where the tears had fallen.

In her stillness, she heard the constant whir of traffic on the interstate only a few blocks from her bedroom window. She heard the cars, trucks, and buses moving swiftly through the city on what local Atlanta residents call the 75/85 Connector. She brought her eyes up from the page of her journal when she peered out from her window and observed the traffic. Atlanta was her city now, and she had come to love it, even after swearing she would never move here over a decade ago. Falling in love with Atlanta had become a process, a subtle one that happened over time after she had accepted her internship at the law firm that still writes her paychecks. As she continued to watch the vehicles streaming through the city, she remembered one of her favorite quotes. "The only way through is through." It was a quote she recited a hundred times over and the battle cry she used to get through the hardest season of her life—Mimi's sudden death. Still overcome with grief, the only way through it was through it. She knew that with any process, like falling in love with Atlanta, there were no shortcuts to the good stuff. The only option was to move through, evolving as the process progressed.

Taking her eyes back to her tear-stained journal entry, she picked up a pen once again and began writing her thoughts. Maybe the goal wasn't for her to find her way back to the place she was when Mimi was still alive. Maybe the goal was to create a legacy of her own. Maybe she was supposed to find her own passion and a torch to carry herself. Mimi enhanced Bianca's understanding with exposure to the realities of what black men faced every day in our country, but she needed to find her own reason to fight. She needed to build her own relationships. She needed to understand the suffering of others. She had to arrive at the point of being tired of giving in.

Bianca had no idea where to start, but she knew Mimi had

planted a seed deep in her soul, and with intention and effort, she could find it again. Although the task felt daunting and was indeed overwhelming, Bianca felt relieved. She finally caught her breath and exhaled deeply. No matter how far she strayed, she was still Mimi's granddaughter, and that gave her hope. In the painful emotions Bianca felt that evening, hope was hard to detect, but it was there, almost hidden, barely detectable, and yet undeniably powerful as a source of sustaining energy to not give up at any time in the fight. Bianca reached across her chair for her brown leather briefcase and pulled out her personal computer. She opened a spreadsheet, wrote, "History of Black Americans" at the top, and clicked over to the internet browser. For a second, she paused, stared at the screen, and did not know where to begin her own learning process about racial injustice. Bianca stood at the base of a Kilimanjaro-sized mountain, peered up at the task of exposing herself to the plight of black people in America over the past four hundred years and sensed it would be a lifelong journey to arrive at the top.

She knew the only way to climb the mountain was to trek up one step at a time. She knew so little about the black struggle that she wanted to devote herself to it as an advocate, the way Mimi had done all her life. Lack of knowledge was embarrassing. She didn't like to feel ignorant. Pride made it hard to admit she didn't know. If left to simmer for too long, pride would get in the way of learning if she didn't start now. She had to start right now, somewhere, anywhere. She typed "History of Black Americans" in the search engine toolbar and clicked on the first article where she read stories of survivors from the Underground Railroad.

After reading, Bianca captured the link on her spreadsheet, determined to capture her notes as she learned. She thought about the plight of the travelers on the Underground Railroad and pondered how powerful hope can be, even if it's a tiny, imperceptible amount. The slaves who escaped to the North faced ugly external forces that robbed them of their freedom. Bianca faced ugly internal forces that robbed her of her ability to advocate for her fellow Americans of different skin colors. She took a serious and sincere note of hope's powerful force in the lives of the escaping slaves. Bianca understood she must hang on to her own shred of hope. Like a seed buried under the surface of the soil, it is unseen but still a powerful force for growth and change. Hope buried, but working.

Her underground hope.

## ABOUT VIRGINIA

Virginia is a writer, mother of two, and ministry leader in a multi-racial church. She uses knowledge from a decade-long writing career and her family's mission "to be a beacon of hope" to bring Bianca's story to life in Underground Hope. As a white woman who grew up in a predominantly white community and now lives in a predominantly black one, Virginia leverages her own experience to shine a beacon of hope into Bianca's hopelessness, as she faces her own role in racial injustice. You can access more writing content and contact Virginia personally at www.virginialeefortunato.com.

## ACKNOWLEDGEMENTS

To Lukas, my biggest cheerleader and Mom and Dad, who come in a very close second, thank you for your relentless belief in me. To my church and neighborhood, thank you for being brave enough to let me love you imperfectly.

# story seven

# THE TRUTH ABOUT YOU

## MARTHA JEIFETZ

*I* grew up in Buenos Aires, the capital of Argentina. It is a large, modern, and cosmopolitan city that some would compare to other international destinations such as Madrid or Paris. Yet, there is a singularity to Buenos Aires as it feels always busy, unapologetically loud and vibrantly alive. There is the constant noise from the buses, transporting people at all times of the day and night, as well as dense fumes coming from everywhere that add to the intense smog that usually overwhelms one's senses. There is also the *clank, clank, clank* sound of small shops opening their aluminum curtains to welcome the opportunities and hopes of the day while shouting good morning to neighbors and passing by customers. Buenos Aires is busy, almost restless, and yet amid all of this, we are reminded to take deep breaths and find our way forward.

Taking deep breaths is not a privilege I take for granted, particularly since my mother only carried me for seven months. My parents described me as a multi-tasker years before people even understood the meaning of the word because I had the ability to do a great number of things simultaneously and well. Perhaps the most remarkable of my talents were the skills of organization and tidiness. I remember my mom repeatedly telling the same story about how when I was three or four years old she dressed me in white clothes and sent me to the park with my dad and my sister. I sat on a bench and read a book and even played in the sandbox for hours, but still managed to come back home happy and spotless. I have always been calm, organized, and strong-willed. That is, until I met Irma.

I do not remember exactly when she came into my life. I cannot recall the precise moment that she made her official and bold appearance. The things I remember are her strong presence and the profound impact she had on me. Sometime during the fall of 1983, Irma made her existence felt for the first time in the beautiful area of the Argentine Patagonia, full of trees and very lush foliage. I never knew a lot about her or her family, as she rarely shared personal information. I guess she had a lonely childhood and, because her parents worked a lot, she was often *watched-sat* by humble and caring people. They were the type of caregivers who would follow along with her games and would try to protect her at all costs from any potential harm.

Irma was about 5'7 tall and had long, silky dark coffee-colored hair. Her round, deep, hazelnut-colored eyes seemed inviting and innocent at the same time. She reminded me of a skinny and beautiful eucalyptus tree. These kinds of trees are allelopathic, as they quickly absorb nutrients and water from the soil and leave other plants thirsty and malnourished. Branches that extend from their medium-width trunk are filled with evergreen leaves that are lanceolate-shaped and have a glossy green look. Eucalyptus tree branches give them the ability to reach any height with a soft, almost imperceptible touch. The tree is a symbol of strength and protection, and it is known for its survival skills and its nature of eradicating other native plants. They defend their territory by using their roots to draw more water from the soil, preventing other plants from growing.

And so it was with Irma. The first thing people noticed about her was her strong presence, especially her robust fragrance, a minty, pine scent with a touch of honey much like eucalyptus. Although I could smell her coming, she moved gracefully like a ghost nearly gliding across any room and making me feel uncomfortable and out of my own element.

Irma grew up playing alone, and over time she started exploring brain games, such as crossword puzzles, quizzes, and word problems all of which gave her the chance to sharpen her thoughts and improve her memory, attention, focus, and brain speed. She became an expert at using words to influence others with her ideas. Irma had a bright imagination that she used along with her creativity and over-protectiveness to get what she wanted all the time. She would play the victim role with her sitters and even her parents. I watched her win almost impossible negotiations with her parents and teachers with finesse and ease. One of her tactics was spotting a hole in an idea, contorting it and convincing an adult to move otherwise. She could also persuade people that she was innocent and disadvantaged in virtually every situation. I have lost count of the number of times she made me lose confidence in myself. I was a great student, and yet, Irma made me believe my grades were never good enough. It was in high school when her allelo-pathic-like true nature really began to become visible to me.

During high school, I spent most of my time listening to and hanging on to her words. She was jealous of my friends and hyper-protective of me. She demanded my attention all day. She couldn't stand me spending time with other people, and oftentimes, she would come up with stories to make me believe others were being mean to me for no reason at all. She would hurl insults at me, reminding me of the things I was not good at or shining a big light on my failures while making little mention of my accomplishments and successes. Why couldn't she celebrate with me when I was selected among hundreds of teenagers to represent the country in a global competition? Why would she make me feel I didn't deserve the honor when I worked so hard for so many months? When I was presented with new opportunities and even promotions at work, I could not celebrate or even talk about them with Irma because in her unique way of looking at life, it was never good enough.

For years, I felt I was under her spell having lost count of the times she convinced me I was not worthy enough for my friends, my family, my job, or even myself. She made me feel meaningless and insecure. And yet, I loved her nonetheless.

She could compel me to believe whatever she said by twisting my own words, making me believe something I would never have thought or said. Numerous times, I thought, "Wait! I never said that. You're putting words in my mouth." But she was always there with me, whether I wanted her to be there or not. I was stuck with her and, oddly, felt the safest in her company.

Irma had a solid voice. Once, she used her tone and only a couple of choice words to destroy my friend Matt's self-confidence in less than five minutes. She didn't say much, but she used the right words in just the right way to make him believe he was unworthy of love and attention. He crumbled to the floor under her voice. I felt hopeless and guilty as I watched the scene unfold. Afterward, she turned to me and asked, "What did I say?" and I was speechless. I could not remember the exact words, but I know for sure that they were deeply hurtful and destructive. It took Matt several years to find the strength to believe in himself again and, more importantly, to trust others.

Irma was a force of nature. I could feel her energy filling my home and my body like a hurricane wind whooshing swiftly across the floors, turning everything in its path upside down with quiet resolve. It felt like her shadow was passing by me, coming from another dimension. To understand Irma's motives is to know the sheer silence and calmness one feels when they are in the eye of a hurricane. You know something powerful is coming, but you are not sure when its impact will strike or how strong it will be. I often wondered why Irma picked me and why she chose to stay with me for so long. More importantly, why did I let her?

Over time, I started to question Irma's intentions. What was it about me that Irma craved so much? My attention? My love? Or perhaps she was simply lonely. I did not know, but as I grew into adulthood, moved to other countries and met new and different people, I began to gain clarity. I developed perspective and recognized that I might have been living in a made-up world. I had believed her stories about me, consumed her lies, and internalized her condescension.

For the first time in my life, I understood it was time for me to have a heart-to-heart conversation with Irma, my oldest friend and confidant. I remember replaying the conversation in my head over and over again, repeating my mentally rehearsed speech, rebutting her objections and every childish reaction I imagined I could possibly encounter. As thoughts tumbled through my head and my heart, I was afraid I might hurt her and make her feel unloved too, but the pain I was in was no longer serving me, and so I knew I had to act quickly. I mustered up the courage one night and confronted her. I didn't know where to start. My heart was pounding hard in my chest. My hands were sweaty and I felt a quiver of panic. I knew she could be waiting and ready to defeat me with her words one more time.

It was the shortest conversation I had ever had in my life. I opened up to her, appealing to our shared time together and trusting that she would listen to me with all her senses, embrace me as an old loving friend and help me move forward. "It is about time and you need to let me go," I said. "Although I'm thankful for all you did for me and for all the difficulties you helped me overcome, I don't need you anymore. I need you to leave me." And right there, it all made sense to me, and I felt like my life was passing by in front of my eyes. I could see my parents and my grandparents, along with their expectations of me. I could see myself doing my best to please everyone in my life so that they would be happy. The perfect daughter, the amazing student, and the highly driven and successful professional were all the roles I felt I needed to cover so I could accomplish other people's ideas. But what about me and what I wanted to achieve in life? How was I listening to my own desires and passions? How was I to be happy with my choices? All these thoughts passed through my head and my body simultaneously, and then it hit me. Irma had served a purpose. She protected me from negative experiences, not meeting other people's expectations, and she kept me out of danger. She also prevented me from being who I truly was and could become. How was I supposed to learn and grow without making mistakes? I remember crying a lot, feeling uncomfortable and free at the same time. It was one of the strangest emotions I've ever felt in my entire life.

Irma was witnessing it all unfolding before her eyes, so she finally had to hear me and pay attention to what I was demanding. She understood her power was no longer there. It was at that moment that her hurricane force that lived inside me disappeared, and, for the first time ever, I could see her eye-to-eye. Her familiar and profound minty smell dissipated and, almost as magically as she came into my life, she was gone. And with that, I started to see clearly what was important to me, who I wanted in my life, and what made me unique, happy, and fulfilled.

I felt a heavy load being lifted from my shoulders. I wasn't feeling sad or teary anymore. Instead, I felt liberated and powerful and found ease in being able to choose what I wanted to do next. It was exhilarating and scary at the same time.

After confronting Irma, I realized her existence made me weaker and more doubtful when I needed to be strong and confident. I also noticed that she lived in my head the entire time. Irma was a made-up figment of my imagination, even though she has always felt so real. It was then that I truly understood the power of my own words and beliefs and knew I could create my own destiny by living on my own terms. And it was right there that I watched the number of possibilities open right before me, allowing me the ability to pick myself and care for what I wanted, to set my own expectations for life and to be completely and utterly aware of my own power of choice every single moment of every single day.

I felt on top of the world, passionate, incredibly alive and ready to embrace my beautiful and imperfect self again and forever.

After years spent in therapy, meditating and reflecting, I can understand how Irma cared for me from a place of love and protection. She shielded me from negative emotions that others would wreak upon me. But as she shielded and protected me, she also inflicted great pain and self-doubt that prevented me from learning from my own mistakes and that blocked me from taking chances and daring to try.

Gratitude now fills my heart where Irma once lived. Today, I am thankful for her existence, her presence, and her company throughout the years. Because of Irma, I was able to survive and overcome many of my life's challenges. Watching her courage made me take some risks and learn from them, grow and feel appreciation for myself and others, and it gave me opportunities to find happiness and love and to fill my days with those people that support me and push me forward.

I might confess that it was a painful and deep journey for me, but it taught me so much about my values and how to build the self-confidence I needed to bring my whole self with me every day. It was my own process of self-discovery to find out how powerful we can all be when we choose ourselves first, when we believe in our capabilities, and when we serve others with love and compassion.

From time to time, I invite Irma back into my life, and on rare occasions, I honestly miss her and the way she made me feel. At times, I allow her to remind me of my own strength and she comes to keep me company, taking the back seat while I drive purposefully towards my goals and dreams. It was through her life that I was able to discover who I truly am. And what an amazing gift she shared with me!

Ultimately, Irma taught me that finding my self-worth is what makes me unique and beautiful. And with that, I can choose to consciously choose to bring my best self with me every day, as we all can. And that is what makes us powerful and gives us the amazing opportunity to create the life we deserve.

## ABOUT MARTHA

Martha Jeifetz is an Executive Coach & Consultant, a mom and a fun, caring and positive human being. She has helped hundreds of leaders around the world for over 25 years to get clarity on their personal and professional goals and take tangible steps to achieve them. Her personal mission is to help and support people to live their best lives by finding practical actions to implement that make their dreams a reality every day. She believes life is worth enjoying to the fullest today. Find more about her at www.mjthecoach.com

## ACKNOWLEDGEMENTS

My wholehearted gratitude for my biggest teacher in life and love, Kyla. To Flavio, for his unconditional support and patience, my parents and siblings that questioned and nourished me in equal parts and my dear friends, colleagues and partners that have loved me and pushed me forward; For the northern light that has somehow always guided me. And Irma. Thank you to all of you that believed in me, for holding me, for seeing the potential, the love and the pain. And lastly, for all the naysayers and critics that made me question who I am. Thank you all for helping me find the truth about me!

# story eight

# THE MARK

## SHAKENNA WILLIAMS

### THE NIGHT BEFORE PICTURE DAY - 1980

"*D*ee, it's time to go to bed!" Mom says with a smile as she peeks her head into my bedroom.

"Yes, Mom!" I respond before turning off the light and jumping into my soft canopy bed. I pull the covers over my head. Now, it is time for us to get back to our often needed conversation. I am not going to let you mess up my picture day like you did last year.

Tomorrow is school picture day and I am filled with anxiety about how you are going to appear. I can usually control how you appear, but school picture day is when our mother will select our look, from outfit to hair-do. It is not the outfit that I am worried about. It is how I will position you.

Our Catholic school has a strict uniform policy. I remember the pride our mother would take in making sure our uniform was pressed and the mandatory round-collared shirt was pearly white. She would wake us up early to style our hair neatly.

As I lie awake dreading Picture Day, my mind flickers like

the steady shuttering of a camera lens. With each click of the camera, I envision a different way to conceal you. The clicking camera in my mind flashes continuously. With each click and each accompanying flash, I picture a new way of trying to hide you. I can hear the photographer telling me to move you to the left, to the right, tilt you up a little bit, and shift you down a tad. My goal on picture day is to ensure you do not take center stage.

> *Me on center stage; how could this be, Dee? Why do you always try to hide me? I am part of you, so WE are on center stage. Every day, especially on Picture Day, I yearn to be accepted as part of your wholeness. Why do you remain fixated on keeping me silent by hiding me? I feel your pain and misery with finding the courage and the right words to justify my existence. I'm sorry about how my presence has caused you so much pain.*

Oh boy, now I really can't sleep! I can feel my heart beating faster and my blood boiling. I have suffered through so much trauma just because of you. The energy it takes to position you correctly for picture day will be downright exhausting. I have so many thoughts about preparing for tomorrow. Will the photographer ask me to introduce you? What outfit or hairstyle will mother select? Perhaps I can convince her to select a style that I want this time.

In the morning, we will walk into the kitchen to see that mother has transformed our kitchen into a hair salon. She is always excited about doing our hair. She will have the brown leather kitchen chair near the electronic stove. Gently placed on the kitchen table will be a variety of colored silk ribbons, barrettes, combs, brushes, and hair grease. With her huge smile, Mother will pat the back of the kitchen chair to motiion for us to sit down. The pressing comb that will be used to straighten our hair will be warming up on the stove. Oh no, I can already smell the odor of burnt hair. How am I going to ask for the style that I need to hide you?

I love my mother's fashion taste, so I am not worried about the outfit she will select. My worry is about you and keeping you hidden. How can I keep you silent? It will take all of my inner strength to stop you from taking the spotlight on Picture Day and my life. UGH!!! Every time I see you, I can hear you saying, "I'm not going anywhere. Remember, YOU promised."

*Yes, the promise you made to our grandmother, Nana. I remember that day, hearing her smooth and calming voice, telling you never to get rid of me. That she thought we were beautiful the way we were born. Do you remember the first time Nana laid eyes on us? She was so excited to see her first grandchild. Mom and Dad were so happy to have their firstborn after years of being married. Finally, we were here! They loved and adored me. Why don't you? I hope I can help you understand how I wanted to be your everything. I did not mean to inflict so much pain on you.*

"Aww... you are right," I think to myself.

The excitement and love we received from Nana and our parents overrode the pain of the words and looks I received when people noticed you. When people address you, they address me. You are me and I am you.

I promised Nana at a very early age that I would never get rid of you. I want to love you as Nana loved us. She taught me that I was beautifully and wonderfully made in God's image. God's creative power to design and match us is beyond comprehension.

Together, our identity is distinct from anyone else's. We are one. It took me years to realize and accept that God had given me something extra. It was you.

*Dee, please understand that I have tried to stay in my place and to be as quiet as possible. I don't remember the first time my presence caused you so much pain.*

*When the doctors and our parents first spotted me, I made a bold statement. You have characterized my unwanted position as being bold, loud, and obnoxious. I do agree in a way. Throughout the years, I have matured, and so have you.*

*Well, go to sleep so we can get some rest.*

I roll over to one side and pull the comforter over my head tightly. Even as I snuggle deeper into the pillow, I still can't sleep, and it's all your fault! All my life, you have had a dominant presence. I feel like people want to meet and get to know you before they meet me. You are very pronounced, although, over the years, you have matured and leveled out your personality. I have never spent the time researching how you became part of me. Usually, you are silent until someone asks about your existence. And then I hear your voice, like an unwanted stranger trying to make conversation.

*I am here and I have been with you since the beginning. I have heard every word, every disrespectful and painful word, blanketed with your guilt and shame over me. People have been cruel with unsolicited and harsh comments about me. Names have meaning and they hurt. It hurt you and it hurt me.*

It's funny, all these years, I have never given you a name or taken it upon myself to find out or even ask mom and dad why you are with me. I just called you "The Mark." You are softly nestled in your domain on the right quadrant of my forehead. When you arrived, you were a raised bubble on my forehead that slowly decreased to become an inconspicuous mark. You are perfectly round, approximately .75 inches in diameter and .75 mm in depth. Your shape has been compared to the likes of a penny. Indeed, your shape is perfectly round with a copper tone. Thank God, your face doesn't resemble President Lincoln. Instead, it is more of an impression of a kiss. That's probably why many of the gentler comments described you as a kiss from God or an angel.

*I agree some of those names did not make sense, such as the penny. A penny has two sides. I'm only visible on one side. Were they referring to me as a penny because of my color? I guess so. Or were they referring to the other side they can't see...you?*

*How about being called 'the scar' from the result of a bullet? How is this possible? How?! Shot right in the head with no other scars? If they only knew the pain I feel when they say I look like a gunshot. It's painful and immobilizing. It really hurts.*

*Now, some of the nicer names, like the Kiss from God or an angel, though nice, still hurt.*

I don't remember the first time someone asked me about you. I can't remember when I felt the pain of words that someone said. Yet, whenever someone asks, "What's that on your head?" The hurt returns. The pain feels like I've been raped mentally of all of my intelligent thoughts, robbed of inner peace, and stabbed with the sword of hatred and insecurity. Their words echo in my head and translate in my brain into one simple thought, "I am ugly."

I have removed so many people out of our lives when they teased or said mean things about you. I would freeze, paralyzed in fear, as if facing an oncoming train. Their comments truly hurt me to the core. At times, I felt breathless, empty and void. Yet, I have come to realize that you have a purpose.

So, why do I want to hide you? By hiding you, I hide your purpose. You are helping expose the true character and ignorance of others. You have always been with me in good and bad times. You don't take up a lot of space. You are just not in the right place. You're unmovable! Learning how to hide you is an ongoing challenge. Why do I want to keep you hidden?

*Dee, what are you saying? I wish I could convince you not to hide me. When you hide me, it makes me hot and sweaty. Every time you part your hair, I say to myself, "Here comes the shade." You have covered me with a full bang or a side part with your hair swooshed over to cover me.*

*The outfit never mattered. Jewelry didn't matter. Yes, it would be cool for someone to compliment our clothes, but it would be nicer if they complimented us. "Geez! I would even take a compliment about our shoes. But nope... Instead, someone always has to go and say something mean about me. That always forces you to internalize the pain.*

*You hold on to their words so tightly, trapping them in your conscious awareness. You give life to their words, but never consider whether they are true. Every time you ask, "why," you question my existence, and that is far from true. Their words only have the value you assign them. You let their consistent teasing create insecurities, anxiety, weakness, and self-polarization while ignoring the reason I exist. I pray that one day you will understand that I make you you. You are me, and I am you.*

But throughout my life, you have caused me so much pain and grief. You make me feel insecure and unsure. The two hardest battles that I have to overcome are hearing what others say about you and living with the painful knowledge that you will always be a part of me. I work so hard to hide you. You embarrass me. Hiding you and trying to find creative ways to explain you is mind-numbing. I'm tired of covering you up. I wish you would disappear. But, if you do, I will disappear as well, and that means I will break my promise to Nana.

*If I had a voice, I would thank Nana for making you promise to never get rid of me. I appreciate her unconditional love.*

*Please don't confuse my position in your life with disdain. Because I am a part of you, I feel all of the love Nana shared with you. Nana always told you that we were beautiful and her love for you and for us was genuine. What made your vow to her so important?*

## THE NIGHT BEFORE PICTURE DAY - 2020

It has taken four decades for me to come to the realization of what a marvelous creation you are to me. Your purpose has played a tremendous role in changing the trajectory of my life. You have transformed me into the strong, bold, and sassy person I am today. You have shaped my personality to want to help others, especially those who are unfortunate, unwanted, and unloved. You have made me humble and given me high emotional and social intelligence to be mindful of others. Looking at us, I see our grandmother. This is why the vow is so important to me, as we are our grandmother. You are me and we are her.

*Yesss! We are more than what people see. There is a gap between how we view ourselves and how others see us. So many have not even acknowledged my existence, while others have exacerbated your feelings of not being beautiful with their harsh words. Somehow, you were able to suppress these feelings by giving a sweet smile rather than hurling back an equally painful remark that reflected your true feelings.*

*I'm proud of how you did not allow those negative remarks to affect your values, passions, aspirations, and reactions to the people who hurt you. You found internal self-acceptance and developed a strong external self-awareness. You have established trusted relationships and personal and social controls, which to me translated into happiness and contentment. Your empathy and consideration of others' perspectives are remarkable. The bottom line is that I love you. I love us.*

I have misunderstood your presence and overlooked your purpose. I denounced your role in my life. I grappled with your existence. The division I have caused between us is senseless. I blamed you for not becoming what I thought I wanted to be or having the relationship I thought I should have. I used you as an excuse for not pursuing my dreams. You are a dominant part of my life, but I still hide you. This self-division is a challenge that I have created within myself. You did not do that. I did. I'm sorry for hiding you. You make me whole.

Having you as part of my journey has made me non-judgmental. Because of you, I have the ability to care for, love, and empower others. I want to give others the love and security you silently gave me. I wish I had reciprocated your love. I now see that I could not love you because I did not fully love myself. This realization pains me more than those who teased you ever could have. How can I make this right?

*I am whimpering with joy. I have long waited for this opportunity for us to discuss your feelings about me. You don't owe me an apology. I have been waiting to say, "Thank you." You have taken and endured so many harsh comments on my behalf. Each time, as painful as it was, you confidently defended me. To me, that is true love. The same love I felt when your parents saw you for the first time. After seven years of marriage, you were finally here! I don't know who asked first, dad or mom, what I was. Quite frankly, it did not matter to them. You and I were a perfect match.*

Self-hate has gotten in the way of my love for you. I portrayed you as my enemy, but I was the adversary. Instead of being proud to have you, I hid you. Masking who you were allowed me to block you from being the center of attention. Your presence has evoked so much pain. I never felt pretty, normal, or accepted. I feel this most when people ask me what you are. But you are me, aren't you?

Everyone is born with something unique about them. You are easy to see and you get noticed for your odd position, shape, size, and definition. You are what makes me unique, precisely crafted, a symbol of God's greatness. You have enhanced my uniqueness and shaped my character. As a dark-skinned black woman, gaining acceptance has been an ongoing challenge; however, accepting you was more painful. I can still hear the ignorant, awful and unkind comments from others echoing in my head. You have helped me become more confident. You have helped me become fearless, brave and bold. You make me who I am.

So, why has it taken me so long to acknowledge you and recognize your beauty? To diagnose what was holding me back was not you, it was me. Or is it us? You are so poised and exotic. Your boldness has attracted many welcome and unwelcome exchanges from those curious about you. This strong and biting reaction has caused so much pain. Did you feel it too? I never asked you how you felt, as you don't speak, you are just there. I feel so weak when someone asks me what you are. You are me, aren't you?

I cannot recall when I had the epiphany that by loving you I could truly love myself, but I'm glad it happened. A choice to love yourself is a successful accomplishment of self-love. Although the emotional toll is not the same as having a mental or physical disability, the pain of feeling ugly and different has long prompted selfish desires to belong.

*I have always wanted you to accept me, Dee. In our life, people have called me many names, but what I have longed for is for you to call me your own. I intrusively became a part of you.*

138

*Scientifically, my existence came from being an unformed blood vessel. Perhaps I should have tried harder to be fully formed, so my presence would not be so pronounced. My inability to form has caused you so much pain.*

*What has formed is a spiritual connection between us, a connection built on a promise to always remain together. My silence was intentional to allow you time to sort through your pain, discover your true feelings of loving yourself and, most importantly, love me and love us. What makes this journey with you exciting is knowing how much you love me and I love you.*

Thank God for Nana for making it possible for me to love you. I never should have questioned why you existed or how you were formed because the love I received from Nana and my parents overrode the pain from those who meant us harm. Our parents and Nana had our best interests in mind and loved us unconditionally.

You need no official name, no identity, as you are me. You are the missing piece of my personal puzzle that I have grown to love.

*Your life's purpose is not to defend me, but I am glad that I have brought you a sense of purpose. You have accomplished a magnificent feat by blocking out negativity and living with positivity. Your acceptance of my love has given me so much joy. I'm honored and proud to be with you. Yes! You are me and I am you.*

I am so grateful I kept my commitment to Nana and did not get rid of you. This means so much. It still hurts when people tease me about you, but their words will never change my love for you. I love you so much. Our mutual love and respect has given me the confidence to achieve and overcome obstacles.

*Aw! What is that noise? It's the buzzing from the alarm. I don't want this conversation to stop, but it's time to get up. Today, we are ready! Thank you for forgiving me. Today is our day to take center stage. Get ready to shine!*

## ABOUT SHAKENNA

Dr. Shakenna "Dee Dee" Williams is an entrepreneur, educator, business connector, financial coach, and diversity, equity, and inclusion implementer. She is passionate about mentoring women and young girls to pursue their life goals with purpose and impact.

Dr. Williams' excerpt, "The Mark," will inspire those challenged with self-love to embrace their unique beauty. Dr. Williams' shares a candid tale of the promise she made to her grandmother. This promise transformed her life, allowing her to find true self-love and acceptance.

To inquire about booking Dr. Shakenna K. Williams for a speaking engagement or workshops, please contact Info@KennaBusinessSolutions.com

## ACKNOWLEDGEMENTS

I would like to thank my Unstuck Writers' Retreat sisters for their encouragement through this writing process.

I want to acknowledge and thank my brother, Michael, for giving me the nickname "Dee Dee." This piece is dedicated to my mother, Lillian, my late father, Douglas, and my late maternal-grandmother, Rebecca "Nana" Savage.

# story nine

# CONSIDERING DADDY

## SHALONDRA E. HENRY

**JUNE 5, 2021, SATURDAY**

*T*he canary yellow, thigh-length dress was perfect for a girl named Lark. Last weekend, Handsome and I spent a hurried afternoon searching for something just right for the occasion. After I mentioned that I was still waiting for an expedited shipment from overseas, he said, "I would like to take you shopping." Yes, he proved again to be an incredibly bright light shining on my otherwise bumpy journey.

And tonight... it was one of the best nights EVER!

On this night, I reclaimed my life and celebrated more passionately than ever. Arriving at this moment was stressful due to my child's father, my sister and my job. All while single mommy-ing. But I remained present in each difficult moment. I maintained focus, knowing that there was light and that this tunnel was not a permanent fixture of my sojourn. I pushed ahead, believing that there was another side. One that is better because it supports my joy as well as my bright and sometimes silly light. Which is what this celebration and party were about.

Me and JOY! Me and LOVE! The joy and love that comes from being seen for all the parts that I bring-the good, the bad, the ugly and indifferent.

Claiming the years in a way that I had not done previously. During all those years in Los Angeles, I mastered concealing my age and wisdom for fear of others judging my path or cordoning off opportunities from my reach. But tonight? I am confident and thankful. This path of mine has a purpose and I am ashamed of nothing. Not one single, solitary thing!

I happily flitted about like a bird free from its cage, only touching down on the experience that served my highest good.

As of late, there were many reasons that I could have felt defeated. Hell, I was defeated, but I just would not accept it. Time and time again, I experienced setbacks and unforeseen obstacles that would WHOOSH into my life and BAM! sucker punch me with an inescapable thud!

However, this evening is not about acknowledging any of that negativity. This evening is a celebration highlighting the beauty of connectivity. I was un-sober, muddling in the purity of adoration and love exhibited by each soul in attendance. As I looked around the beautiful, newly opened rooftop lounge, I saw so many faces of people I loved. Their presence was a reassurance that I was okay.

It was my birthday. And tomorrow I would commemorate the third anniversary of his departure. Isn't it something? One day we are celebrating my birthday, and the next we catapult into mourning. The date listed on the death certificate is June 7th. He tried to hang on. He did not want me to bear that sorrow at a time when I should be celebrating. Death hit him hard, probably much harder than the obstacles I have faced. He was unsuccessful in making it back to the couch, his bed of choice. Instead, he passed out on the wooden floor of the narrow hallway leading to his bedroom and bathroom. He had called me the night before, but I was at dinner celebrating with my mom and her daughter. He left a message that I intended to return that evening; yet, the next day came with a forgotten intention. On the day he died, I remember hurriedly taking my daughter to my mom's so that I could make it to the corporate office for my first day teaching yoga at their facility. We hopped into my car. It was then that I remembered that a call had come from my mom's brother. When I listened to the message, "Your dad... passed out... emergency room," was all I remember.

I wish he was still here. Writing in this journal is one of the ways I am able to keep him with me. As a gift for my birthday, one of my girlfriends sent me a beautiful, glass jar gilded with the word GRATITUDE along with simple, white folded cards to record my thoughts of appreciation. Today, I scribbled on one of the cards:

> *I am grateful to hold him in my heart*
> *without the sour aftertaste of disillusion.*

## 23 APRIL 2006, SUNDAY

I miss my daddy.

We used to be close. We hung out. We fixed cars at his shop. We would serve up drinks at the juke joint he owned. We even went fishing. My dad, for all that he was and was not, was The Man. By all accounts, Daddy was a self-possessed man- unmoved, unbothered, and unapologetic (long before that was a thing).

On days when he wanted to be anonymous and free, he would say, "Let's riiiide" in his southern, macho black man drawl. I knew better than to ask, "Where are we going?" Looking back, somehow I knew there was never really a definitive answer to that question. We were off to wherever the road took us. *Vrrrrrroooom!!* Those drives were not just about escaping the small-town energy of Palm Meadow, but they were also excursions responding to the need for adventure and freedom of the open roads splintering throughout the countryside. We used to fish too. Did I already say that? I loved fishing. I miss those days, those moments shared with him. I wrap myself around those memories because they are so few. Far. And too much in between. Now, as I sit here reminiscing, I would give almost anything to have just one of those moments again.

My dad was an alcoholic. Well, he is an alcoholic. He came home late, raising hell and sometimes waking us up to insist I wash the two dishes left in the sink. He made me so mad. On the nights that I didn't have to be in bed early in preparation for my next day of school, he would find me in blissful solitude on the couch as I read or watched the tube. He would disrupt it by edging me out of the family room and demanding that I go to sleep in my bed so that he could have the couch. He slept there a lot. How dare he decide when and where to enter my life? Didn't he know that I was a voracious reader? How dare he come and go? Red eyes and funky breath, stinking and stinging like a ferocious dragon! Yes, he was a force. There is no doubt about that. But what I really wanted was for him to be consistent, present, loving, supportive, encouraging, and most of all, proud of ME.

My mom always said, "He loves you more than anything." But it wasn't apparent to me. All I felt was his disappointment. I wasn't sure of what to do, though. I guessed that it was in the fact that I wasn't born a male-a counterpart to balance the power in our home. Maybe that is why he didn't spend much time there-too much estrogen and hair grease. My mom secretly gave thanks for that balance. Not because she was a control freak, but because she knew that he would have more sway over the type of person her never-to-be-born son would have turned out to be. Perhaps that testosterone-filled boy would have been too free, too unapologetic, and, what's even more frightening to consider, too rebellious. I guess having daughters was a form of her exerting control. The deafeningly silent warfare they waged left me as an arbiter in two seemingly different worlds: one of good and one of evil. Torn between loving both and feeling compelled to choose.

The anger I have felt has been love responding to betrayal. Parents, I suppose, love their children the best way they know how. I now realize that my mother was correct – he has loved us despite his flaws from the beginning, far beyond my comprehension. I couldn't see it, at least not the way I do now. But I am clear. He has always done the best he knew how.

He was young. I know that he wanted to go away. Escape the trappings of the cocoon and the limitations placed on a maverick spirit with brown skin in the post-Civil Rights American South. He needed to be free, but he chose to answer the call of fatherhood, knowing she wasn't prepared to be his wife. And, he wasn't ready either, but he knew that she was a good girl and deserved more than what her father gave her. He didn't understand how her father could leave, but he did understand why. In the same way, many men understand but choose not to follow the impulse to leave. Depending on how you look at it, it either takes a lot of selfish cowardice or a lot of unselfish courage, or perhaps some of both.

There were times when I would have preferred that he not be present. Many times, I dreamt of scenarios ranging from sudden, tragic death to simple disappearances. In those dreams, I did not see myself as a victim; instead, I was just a little girl whose father was gone. I even imagined wills and insurance policies. Yes, I contemplated those things as a child.

Being such, I didn't understand the intricacies, the mired minutiae, the quandary of adulthood or of life. Now that I am a grown woman, I see those details with more and more clarity. I understand more and more. I relate more and more. I forgive.

Believe it or not, I forgot as well. It's okay because peace comes with the loss of memory. Happiness and joy emerge. More importantly, there is hope.

Yet, our mind's eye is a muthafucker. It is the lens through which we interpret the world and our place in it. It is as delicate and fragile as a kaleidoscope. A revolution of colors, tilting, shapes bending and creating some semblance of reality. The slightest thing can distort it and change the vision forever. Is that good or bad? How do we know? How do we discern? But what I have learned is that what happens next is dictated by how much we can release. Power and control can only be gained by breathing into it, not holding on, constricting, or cursing the movement. Change is constant, and constant is change. That is a lesson we all must learn – the universal truth, a natural law. The real survivors are those who bend and re-invent and change form while not losing their essence. Much like my childhood comic book hero, the Wonder Twin, Wendy, who showed me that being able to morph is a superpower.

## 25 APRIL 2006, TUESDAY

Mom is not an innocent victim. My sister and I were, but not anymore. Mom had choices to make too. If she had been prepared to make self choices or if she had been prepared to make team choices, perhaps things would have been different. Dad wanted us girls to be strong and self-sufficient, never relying on beauty. Mom did too. However, they seem to have had different visions of what that meant. They seem to have differing views of how being strong and self-sufficient mani-fests itself. If only they knew how to attach us – husband to wife, parent to child, sister to sister. If they could have agreed, together, that family was first and child-rearing required a team, perhaps things would have been different. Recognizing this gives me hope for the choices that I may have to make one day as a life mate and as a parent. Even if I never am in their position, I feel better at least thinking that I understand parenting a little better.

With this understanding, there is no longer any blame. It's just life, figuring it out as I go. I have made the best decisions possible. Are they good or bad? Who knows besides God? And I have to ask myself, is the final judge really sitting back keeping score? Perhaps the Almighty is busier doing other things, like trying to help us help ourselves. It's like placing the right person in our path so that we will find more happiness. It's like breathing life into us every day. We are not expecting anything but for us to reach our greatest, divine potential. I don't know. That's what I think the Most Omniscient does every day. I think that is how He, I mean, She, derives pleasure. You know what I'm saying? Every day, God is focused and intent on creating joy within us. But somehow, we... well, possibly most of us, but maybe not you... but we mess it all up. We fight against what is intended, thinking we know better.

## 26 APRIL 2006, WEDNESDAY

I thank God for perspective. Perspective should get capital letter deference. It's just that important. Anyway, I feel like I'm getting more and more of it each day. I'm so happy that I am falling in love with my dad. In a healthy way, I think. He's not the selfish, bastard that I always knew him to be. He's actually a caring dude. He cares for those whom he loves. He doesn't give care out to everyone. It's reserved, as well it should be. We all should be more like him really. Okay, I know, I'm getting a little carried away. The point is he's a man, a person, who is figuring his pathetic existence out just like many other people attempt to figure themselves out. My problem is that I have been sitting in judgment of how he connects to the world which is different than I do. Yet, I love him and I will protect him. Is that weird that I am compelled to defend him? And from who? Me?

One of my favorite (it used to be my most embarrassing) moments with him is when he picked me up from elementary school in his red, old-school Army Jeep. He had the top-off with the doors completely removed. I always loved cruising open country roads in that Jeep, with freedom carried in each breeze. I enjoyed feeling the excitement of the air bouncing playfully on my skin, encouraging my hair to flitter about and tickle my nose. That particular day, I was not prepared for the heightened experience to come. There was a steep slope that led from the school building to the playground. For generations, Dad's family owned the adjacent property. My grandmother's backyard was littered with fallen pecans from the massive and deeply rooted tree that butted up against the edge of the play area. So, instead of taking the normal route that everyone else's parents took, down the sidewalk-lined driveway to the main road, my dad decided to exit stage right. Which meant down the bumpy hill, through the metal playscape I had played on earlier, and into and through his mom's backyard. I was a mix of terrified nerves and utter disgrace. Yep, I said it - disgrace. We were the freaks that flew down the hill. The rabble-rouser who took the path no one had ever taken. The irreverent and reckless duo that snubbed all the rules of convention. I was the kid who followed all the rules and called on those that didn't. Ugh!!! I didn't know if I would die from embarrassment or from lack of doing the right thing. Now, I look back on it as one of the best experiences I ever had with him. As an adult who understands a bit more about how the world turns, I appreciate his irreverence. However, that type of personality doesn't fare well in a small, southern town. That type of personality opens a juke joint with no liquor license, doesn't pay taxes, pisses off the local officials, and gets taken in by the Georgia Bureau of Investigations. Who knows if he had moved us to Denver as he desired, whether it would have been better for him or for us?

## 30 APRIL 2006, SUNDAY

"I love my daddy. I respect him. He was a bit of a loner, but he always had a job. He's an entrepreneur."

In a dream, I imagined myself being interviewed by Oprah, responding to her questions about my home life. Hearing Cassidy's "I'm a Hustla" as a soundtrack in the background.

Conversationally, I return to answering her questions.

**Me:** Yes, it was always something new. No get-rich-quick schemes or anything like that. He just wanted to find a little peace. He always talked about moving to Denver.

Then we hear the echoing voiceover: "Go (go... go... go...) West, young man (man... man... man)!" [Dreams are so weird.] The interview continues...

**Me:** I don't really know what it was about moving to Denver. I think he sought the solitude that a man gets when he hunts and stakes new territory.

He really is a good man, just unable to fully self-actualize. What does that mean, anyway? Ya know, I don't know exactly, but I'm trying to do it. Sounds like good stuff, huh? Action, active, making shit happen. Can I say that on TV?

(I laugh nervously, while seriously pondering my words, beginning to get lost in my head and then beginning to come back).

**Me:** Making it happen for the Self... I don't know. But it does sound good.

I end with a cheesy, slightly uncomfortable smile, wondering if my thoughts are translating.

**Oprah:** (nods her head knowingly)

With relief that I am communicating clearly, I continue:

I've always said that he and my mom are like night and day. I've always given her a lot of credit, but as I think more about it, perhaps she was the one holding him down, holding him back. She was a small-town girl with class and finesse, but she was too scared to break the mold, too afraid to self-actualize herself. Whatever that means."

"Her Self was so tied to the drama of her mother's life. She was raising her mama's children but wanted to escape at the same time. Escape to the strength, bravado, and seemingly fearlessness of my father's independence and muscular arms."

"I wonder what dating was like for them? Mama, the good girl with the cigarette, made grown because she was a mama before her cherry was ever popped. Daddy the rebel with a misunderstood cause, hidden in a puzzle."

The interview ends.

If you're lucky, with age comes peace. The peace of struggle dismantles and dissipates. The peace of knowing you are done and it is what it is. If you could take some of it back, you would, but you have come to understand that you can't. But knowing you did some good... doesn't that make it all worth it in the end?

Dad knew his fate was staying in The P (I love calling Palm Meadow that... someday it's going to catch on! LOL). He knew just like I did as I watched him become more and more resentful. Loving his babies, but not knowing how. Searching for what was good in himself. You know, many of us have that same search. We want to believe in the all-elusive ME.

The souls of most people surface a little bit at a time, much like an archaeological find. We know something is there, and we have hope that it will be a treasure. But none of us really know. Some people dig and dig until there's nothing left, and they end up eroding what was once something. Touching and manipulating it with no patience, until the soul is ruined, literally for life. I think they call that self-de-actualization, right? The soul is no longer there. And if it is, it is a distortion of the original masterpiece.

## 1 MAY 2006, MONDAY

Why is it that sometimes all you want is to have someone caress your face and smooth your hair as you wake in the morning? Give you a kiss and say something sweet, like "Have a great day, beautiful" or "You're a superstar." Or, something encouraging like, "This is your day and we are all so happy that you are here to be a part of it."

## 2 MAY 2006, TUESDAY

Daddy,

I know life gets hard sometimes, but I like it when you're sober. I feel closer to you. Like we connect. I might know and understand you. Don't be scared. I'll be there for you. I know no one else really has. I don't know what happened to you with your Mama and Daddy, but they did the best they knew how, just as you have. I know it doesn't make it any better, but you gotta' know that they loved you. That she loves you. Yeah, she might be a bitch. I can't really speak to that, but don't let her ignorance get to you. Love yourself the way she couldn't; the way she didn't know-how. So love yourself so that her pain will not be in vain. Love yourself the way that you thought mom would have. Miss Prim and Proper Goody-Two-Shoes wasn't who you thought she would be, was she? Or was she? Take from the heavens what you couldn't get, give to yourself what you wanted and never got. That's what I've done. And can I tell you, it's made a world of difference. I'm happy. I'm not saying that I don't get lonely sometimes or that I don't want someone to love me, but what I'm saying is that even in those times, I'm okay. Emotionally, the world is opening up like never before. Oh, don't get me wrong, I still have my issues. I mean, you can't get rid of years' worth of grime and buildup without working relentlessly. And sometimes, I do get tired. When that happens, I take a break. But I know that the sooner I get back to work, the quicker I'm gonna be able to be clean and sparkly, almost like new. I aspire to be like one of those old houses, full of character and charm but weathered in a comfortable way, content with being one of a kind. Yep, that's what I want.

## 9 MAY 2006, TUESDAY

Every day gets better and better. Why? Because I love my daddy. So simple, it's sad. Is sad really the right word? I have a daddy. What a pleasure to say and feel. I do feel like there has been time lost, but there is no spilt milk here. Only steps forward.

## 18 MAY 2006, THURSDAY

Who am I and how do I contextualize myself? If I don't know myself, how do I know others? The tug of war between being, being seen, and being known leads to frustration about what I want to be known for. Then come the questions: "Who do I want to know me and how much can they know? Where does the danger lie? What is the danger?"

Vulnerability

Pain

Hurt feelings

The list literally can go on and on!

Life is difficult. At least, that's what my Mama says.

The more comfortable I am with myself, the less I need someone else, especially a man, to like me or give me validation or approval. The more approval and validation I feel from my father, the less I need to be anything else other than me: free, loquacious, light, insightful. I am becoming more and more aware of the things that I don't need as well as those that I do.

The interesting thing that I'm finding is that the more in touch I become with my father, the less connected I am to my mother. Something is odd about that. Perhaps, the world is balancing out. Maybe that's why I'm no longer off my axis, tilting on the edge of insanity. Maybe. Equilibrium equals independence. Is independence life or liberation? Or neither.


## 28 JUNE 2006, WEDNESDAY

My dad has become more and more human. I forgive him for all of his inadequacies. What's the point of not forgiving? I mean, really, who does that help? What function does it serve? Forgiving him allows me to forgive life, myself, and those around me. I do wonder, though, how others process life and are able to progress when they are not as enlightened as I am. I sort of laugh while saying this, but I really am serious. Are they living in their own contrived reality in order to get through? A friend once posited that almost everyone is on drugs. When she initially said it, I thought it was an extreme theory. But as I think about it now, I bet that this is how most of us get through. Whether those drugs are over- the-counter, prescribed or street pharmacy. Folks are not looking for happiness, they are looking for escapism through manufactured coping.

I believe that being happy (as in happy beings) is possible. But I sometimes ask myself, if I feel happy, is that all that matters? Is it? Or is there some reality that must be reckoned with to truly be happy and self-actualized? I don't know. I sigh. What is the quest? My quest is to be happy. What is happiness? (So circular, so exhausting. But I can't help myself.)

Happiness for me is having positive relationships with family and friends. What does it mean to have positive relationships? I would like relationships that have some depth. A connection that seeps into the soul and infuses it with motivation and inspiration. Happiness also means laughing, a lot! I mean, a whole lot! It means being with others who are light in spirit and robust in the soul. I really do not enjoy spending time with people who are not. Happiness is freedom. Financial freedom helps, but just feeling unburdened by trivialities in life... now that's the real lightness of spirit.

I wonder if my dad is truly happy.

I wonder what that means for him. Perhaps I will ask him. If I ask, he will give me a roundabout response. That's what he does. When he's uncomfortable with a question, he dodges it-- big time! I suppose many of us do, including myself. We deflect.


23 JULY 2006, SUNDAY

I've always worked toward creating stability for myself and for those around me, particularly my mom, my sister, and my girl-friends. I create and create while at the same time attempting to be free. I try to prove I'm good enough and smart enough. I hope I'm pretty enough. Truly, I just want to find a place I can call home. I've been looking for it, but I now know it's right here with me. It's been here the whole time. I just want to be happy. I want to experience love, give love, take care of myself and share myself. Why is it so hard to do that? I just want lots of laughter and joy. I don't want to be tied down. I want stability, but at the same time, it scares me. It scares me to trust it, to rely on it. My mother was stable. I just want to be normal as in fun, emotional and light. I want to travel. I want to contribute. I want peace. This is a city full of seekers – The City of Angels feels more like the City of Angles being perpetrated by imposters. I don't want to be seeking any longer.

I want a family. I want my family.

I WANT TO BE SEEN!

Loved.

Appreciated.

Protected.

Desired.

Cherished.


## 30 JULY 2006, SUNDAY

I am okay. I am supported. I am smart. I am loved. I trust myself. I am narrowing my focus. I am working on my insecurity. I really need to call my daddy.


## 24 NOVEMBER 2006, FRIDAY

Desperation is the word of the day because I'm at the point at which the need to survive takes over. I wonder if Daddy ever felt desperate. What decisions did he make in those moments? The true measure of a person comes at those times, right? When you are desperate for attention, for love, to be seen, to be heard, or to find a place called home, you may do things that are unspeakable. Or at best, it doesn't sit right in your spirit. Perhaps we all have issues with our fathers to some degree. No experience is held alone, singularly or individually. There can be no action, good or bad, that is held only by one. As much as we feel isolated, none of us are.

## 20 DECEMBER 2006, WEDNESDAY

Letting go of the pain is not easy. It's layered. Done today. Numb tomorrow and hopeful the day after that. It's hard to believe that sitting in the stench of a diseased, decayed dynamic of a relationship isn't always enough to be absolute. Resolved, even for those that have more clarity, does it really dissolve and fade into the waves of the ocean, or is it always there? Waiting like a sleeper cell to be activated.

We are moments away from putting self-inflicted heartache and turmoil into motion. The depth of sadness from the illusion of loss versus the liberation and light that are discovered in the intentional ex-hallllllle.

With a lifted heart, I will breathe.

## ABOUT SHALONDRA

A lover of words and creativity, Shalondra began writing at an early age, publishing her first book, *The Boring Book*, chronicling all things uninteresting in first grade. Since then, her writing has taken many forms, both professionally and personally, writing for television and film projects as well as poetry and short stories. Shalondra is blessed to call two amazing people her daughters and lives in Atlanta, Georgia.

## ACKNOWLEDGEMENTS

I am grateful to God for the following people seeing and believing in me: Shani Godwin and the Unstuck Writers, Judy Hammack, Sandra Robinson, Marilyn Hayes, Parker Henry-McNeil, Kylah McNeil, ShaJra Austin, Sean Reaves, and Dr. Dexter Page.

## ABOUT THE PUBLISHER

An accomplished entrepreneur, author, blogger, podcaster and speaker, Shani Godwin is the founder of Audible Voices, LLC, a boutique publishing company based in Atlanta, GA. Through Audible Voices, Shani helps aspiring authors find their voice and speak their truth as she supports them on their journey to becoming published authors with coached-writing programs and intimate writing retreats.

Shani lives in Atlanta, GA where she enjoys writing, reading, traveling abroad and spending time with family, friends and her fur baby, Zuri Skye.

To learn how you can become a part of The UNSTUCK Writers Collective, please email us at info@audiblevoices.com

CPSIA information can be obtained
at www.ICGtesting.com
Printed in the USA
LVHW040940311221
707391LV00001B/4